The Weather Fifteen Years Ago

Studies in Austrian Literature, Culture and Thought
Translation Series

General Editors:

Jorun B. Johns
Richard H. Lawson

Wolf Haas

The Weather Fifteen Years Ago

Translated by Stephanie Gilardi
and
Thomas S. Hansen

Afterword by
Thomas S. Hansen

ARIADNE PRESS
Riverside, California

Ariadne Press would like to express its appreciation to the Bundesministerium für Unterricht, Kunst und Kultur for assistance in publishing this book.

.KUNST

Translated from the German
Das Wetter vor fünfzehn Jahren
© 2006 Hoffmann und Campe Verlag, Hamburg

Library of Congress Cataloging-in-Publication Data

Haas, Wolf.
[Das Wetter vor fünfzehn Jahren. English]
The weather fifteen years ago / Wolf Haas ; translated by Stephanie Gilardi and Thomas S. Hansen ; afterword by Thomas S. Hansen..
p. cm. -- (Studies in Austrian literature, culture, and thought.
Translation series)
ISBN 1-57241-166-1 (alk. paper)
I. Title

PT2708.A17W4813 2009
831'.92--dc22

2008052505

Cover Design
Beth A. Steffel

270 Goins Court
Riverside, CA 92507

Printed in the United States of America.
ISBN 978-1-57241-166-1

Day One

BOOK REVIEW: Mr. Haas, I've been going back and forth for a long time about where I should start.

WOLF HAAS: So have I.

BOOK REVIEW: Unlike you, though, I don't want to start at the end. Actually –

WOLF HAAS: Strictly speaking, I don't start at the end either. I start with the first kiss.

BOOK REVIEW: But in a way that's the whole point of the story you're telling. Or, the way I see it, the goal toward which everything moves. Speaking strictly chronologically, it belongs at the end of the story. Your hero has been working toward this kiss for fifteen years, and in the end he finally gets it, but you don't describe this scene at the end. Instead, you prefer to put it right at the opening.

WOLF HAAS: There were actually a few openings I liked better. My problem wasn't so much the beginning, or how I should start, but where to put the kiss. You can't just stick it at the end, where it belongs, so to speak. But that would be intolerable. When someone has been waiting for, or as you say, working toward, a kiss for fifteen years, and then he finally gets it, how are you supposed to describe that?

BOOK REVIEW: While I was reading, I wondered if you were declaring war on the reviewer by moving the conclusion to the first page.

WOLF HAAS: That would have been pushing it too far.

BOOK REVIEW: Authors often complain bitterly that reviews give the whole plot away in advance.

WOLF HAAS: That's why I don't write thrillers anymore. It tends to take the edge off if you know everything beforehand. With regular books, I think it helps. It's like teamwork. The blurb and the critics tell the story up front so the author can concentrate on the fine print.

BOOK REVIEW: Good, then let's stay for a moment on the topic of "fine print," as you call it. Your description of this first kiss at the beginning is very detailed – not to say meticulous.

WOLF HAAS: Strictly speaking it isn't the first kiss, but the kiss during which they were both interrupted fifteen years ago.

BOOK REVIEW: Right.

WOLF HAAS: Because you just said meticulous.

BOOK REVIEW: This meticulous, almost pedantic style that your first person narrator uses to describe the kiss he finally gets characterizes him neatly on the first page.

WOLF HAAS: Well, I don't know. I've heard that a lot, that compliment, I guess, that you feel intimately acquainted with Mr. Kowalski through his description of the kiss. If that's how it comes across, it's fine with me.

BOOK REVIEW: He doesn't describe the kiss that he's been waiting for in a particularly romantic way. It's almost technical.

WOLF HAAS: I wouldn't necessarily say technical.

BOOK REVIEW: Matter-of-fact?

WOLF HAAS: I'm not so sure. It's always a little difficult, I find, as an author, being praised for a particular passage.

BOOK REVIEW: You don't like praise?

WOLF HAAS: Of course! But not for the wrong reason. I don't think this kiss on the first page necessarily characterizes him all that well. One critic borrows from another, and pretty soon, it's all over the place that the guy kisses "mechanically" or "matter-of-factly" right from the beginning. Aha! And he's an engineer! How typical of an engineer, the way he kisses. He's been working toward the kiss for fifteen years, and there's also something so nitpicky and uptight about that, and the author stuck all that right on the first page. Good literary kiss craftsmanship, so to speak.

BOOK REVIEW: How is it then for you? Not matter-of-fact, not mechanical –

WOLF HAAS: Well, if it has to be classified, I would call it passionate!

BOOK REVIEW: Excuse me? I'm sorry, but "passionate" would really be the last word I'd use to describe that kiss.

WOLF HAAS: Well, he waited fifteen years for this kiss! And then he finally gets it! If that's not romantic, then I don't know what is.

BOOK REVIEW: But you don't describe as excitingly as you're presenting it to me now. Quite the opposite, actually. The first sentence of the book reads: "If you go a centimeter down from the outer corner of the eye, you come to the cheekbone."

WOLF HAAS: So?

BOOK REVIEW: Then your narrator says "I" for the first time.

WOLF HAAS: Aha.

BOOK REVIEW: And to get more precise, in the second sentence: "More specifically I refer to the left half of the face, to the outer corner of the left eye. If you move a centimeter down from here, you reach the left cheekbone."

WOLF HAAS: And there it is! That's where Anni kissed him!

BOOK REVIEW: Not quite. First you have to go down another centimeter. He says: "And then, one more centimeter straight down, that's where Anni kissed me."

WOLF HAAS: Of course I understand why people say his character is meticulous and pedantic, when he describes a kiss so geometrically, in a straight line and so on. But he also says: I can still feel it now. The location is so important because he still feels the kiss! After hours! He'd been working toward the kiss for fifteen years, and now a few hours have passed since Anni said goodbye to him. Well, it's only until tomorrow, but the reader doesn't know that yet. At this point we only know that she left. But the kiss is still there!

BOOK REVIEW: We only know that she said “bye-bye.”

WOLF HAAS: Yes, she said “bye-bye” and gave him the kiss on the cheek. And now, even though he’s been alone again for another few hours, he still feels the kiss. It burns on his cheek.

BOOK REVIEW: Two centimeters below the left eye.

WOLF HAAS: But he’s in a terrible panic that the kiss he’s waited for all these fifteen years could fade away or even completely disappear. He wants it to linger, so he tries to hang on to the feeling. He needs this exact description – a centimeter in a straight line – to be sure of exactly where he feels it. It doesn’t replace the feeling; he just wants to protect the kiss, sort of.

BOOK REVIEW: Until he sees Anni again the next day.

WOLF HAAS: At least that’s what she promised. Tomorrow I’ll come again, she said after the kiss. He doesn’t dare move because he’s afraid he might lose the kiss.

BOOK REVIEW: He’s making the most of it.

WOLF HAAS: I do see it that way, actually. This is the reason for that “meticulous” description on the first page.

BOOK REVIEW: Because other than that, Anni hasn’t done anything with him.

WOLF HAAS: You can't say it like that. Now you're the one who's being mechanical.

BOOK REVIEW: I am?

WOLF HAAS: When you say "do something" it almost sounds a little pornographic. "Let's do something" or whatever. See, if they wanted to "do something" you wouldn't say he was so uptight and pedantic. But saving a kiss overnight so it doesn't disappear right away, so the kiss stays right where she put it, that's surely the mark of a "meticulous character."

BOOK REVIEW: Now you're twisting my words. "Do something" wasn't meant to be pornographic.

WOLF HAAS: It's true, of course. She really didn't do much. Kiss on the cheek and *ciao*. Before she went, though, she smiled shyly and wiped the lipstick off.

BOOK REVIEW: "Three very quick dabbing motions from the outside to the inside, from ear to nose, parallel to the imaginary extension of my left eyebrow," Mr. Kowalski tells us.

WOLF HAAS: But he points out she didn't brush the kiss away with it, just the lipstick.

BOOK REVIEW: She even rubbed the kiss in.

WOLF HAAS: (*laughs*) Yes, that's actually my favorite part of the whole book. The way he gets the lipstick wiped off, there's something in that. As a man, you know it so well. There's something just really … ambiguous about it, a blend of tenderness and condescension.

BOOK REVIEW: I'm really glad I don't wear lipstick then. He also says: quick dabbing motions. That sounds almost aggressive.

WOLF HAAS: But he only expresses this suspicion so he can dismiss it, reject it. Anni's gesture was meant to be the opposite of aggressive.

BOOK REVIEW: He says: "With quick dabbing motions the 'how' is always important. And it always depends on the 'who.' And it depends on the shy smile. And it depends on the *I'll visit you again tomorrow.*"

WOLF HAAS: Yes, and then the story really begins. The kiss was just a kind of prelude.

BOOK REVIEW: So, now that brings me finally to my beginning.

WOLF HAAS: Oh, so the stuff that came before didn't count?

BOOK REVIEW: Not quite. I'd like to begin with a different question. We know how the novel begins, but what interests me is how the whole story began for you personally. When did you happen upon it for the first time? How did you hit upon it?

WOLF HAAS: That's all very easy to answer. I saw Mr. Kowalski for the first time during his television appearance.

BOOK REVIEW: So, before you knew anything about Anni.

WOLF HAAS: Before I knew anything about Anni or

about him. It was just regular TV. I don't have a TV because I'm prone to television addiction. When I have one, I watch all kinds of garbage. But giving it away just led to my inviting myself over to my friends' houses to watch TV. And when I'm with my girlfriend, I'm permanently glued to the television. Then of course there's a fight because she doesn't understand why I watch things like *Place Your Bets.*

BOOK REVIEW: You watch that, really?

WOLF HAAS: Yes. I admit I really do enjoy it. I just like watching it.

BOOK REVIEW: And on *Place Your Bets* this contestant came out who hadn't been back to his vacation spot in Austria for fifteen years.

WOLF HAAS: "His" vacation spot is a bit of an exaggeration. His parents went there every year. He was just a kid then. They actually carted him off, summer after summer, from birth to age fifteen.

BOOK REVIEW: Fifteen years ago, at the age of fifteen, was the last time he was there.

WOLF HAAS: Yes, that's right. I thought about changing his age slightly so that it wouldn't be confusing. Fifteen years ago and at the age of fifteen. He was thirty at the time of his appearance as a contestant on TV, but naturally I didn't know all that at the time.

BOOK REVIEW: And you were fascinated by him immediately?

WOLF HAAS: No, I wasn't fascinated by him at all.

Just by the challenge. He was a pretty unremarkable person, really the opposite of an interesting or charismatic guy. I'd have to say, a pretty pale character.

BOOK REVIEW: Pale in the truest sense of the word.

WOLF HAAS: Yeah, a little bland. You almost want to say, he doesn't even have red hair. And judging by his skin type, he very well could.

BOOK REVIEW: Now you're being mean.

WOLF HAAS: I'm not trying to be mean. I like pale complexions fine. You couldn't see it very well on TV because of all the makeup, but strangely enough, you could make it out anyway.

BOOK REVIEW: His aura.

WOLF HAAS: His whole body language is that way. On the one hand he seems much older than thirty, but at the same time he's also somehow childlike. Maybe that even intensified the effect of the game show. I immediately got the impression that there must be some crackpot story behind his bet.

BOOK REVIEW: Were you immediately suspicious that someone would study the weather in his vacation spot?

WOLF HAAS: What do you mean, the weather in his vacation spot! The guy lives in the Ruhr and knows what the weather was like on every single day of the past fifteen years in some Austrian mountain village. Although in all these years he hasn't returned to the place even once.

BOOK REVIEW: Right, but on this program there are lots of obscure challenges.

WOLF HAAS: True. I would never have been suspicious if he'd known the weather in his own area for the past fifteen years, although I have to say I think that's also pretty wonderful. That someone even pays attention to the weather of the past. The weather is the kind of thing you're only interested in to know how it's going to be tomorrow.

BOOK REVIEW: Always thoroughly future-oriented.

WOLF HAAS: But how was the weather yesterday, or fifteen years ago? No moron is interested in that, except to compare it to the present. Oh, and maybe the apocalypse freaks who think everything's going to hell and stuff. Or from some important historical event, the temperatures during some campaign, or the sweat stains when Kennedy got shot.

BOOK REVIEW: Nonetheless. It wasn't just the passion for bygone weather that awakened your interest.

WOLF HAAS: That in itself might have impressed me, but not for longer than – a few minutes, maybe. Or for as long as the show lasted, or at the very most until the next day, when I could tell somebody about it.

BOOK REVIEW: For you the crucial factor, then, was that it was a vacation spot in Austria?

WOLF HAAS: No, I didn't give a damn about that! Far from it. All this Austrian baggage is beginning to weigh on me. Wherever I go, the whole country from Vienna to Bregenz goes with me.

BOOK REVIEW: Where's Bregenz?

WOLF HAAS: In Switzerland.

BOOK REVIEW: All right then, what was the crucial thing for you?

WOLF HAAS: It fascinated me that it was the vacation spot of his childhood. And I also have to say that I come from a little Podunk tourist town myself. I know it so well. The love stories, if you can call them that, which start up between tourists and locals, especially when someone comes back to the same place every year. It's the same routine. A few weeks every summer. There's something erotic about that, the waiting, the longing, the dreaming. With kids there's also the added growth spurts, if you're seeing each other only every so often.

BOOK REVIEW: Did you sense right away that there was a love story behind it? On the show he didn't mention anything about that.

WOLF HAAS: Let's just say I hoped so.

BOOK REVIEW: Did you also experience something like that yourself once?

WOLF HAAS: Unfortunately not, but I did have myself in mind when I jumped on this
story. Out of jealousy, sort of. Or as compensation. Who knows? It's an important motivation for writing a book – that you yourself never experience anything.

BOOK REVIEW: But you were pretty active at the time. In any case, you immediately drove up to the Ruhr to meet the man.

WOLF HAAS: Well, “immediately” is an exaggeration. But all things considered, I must admit I was surprisingly active. Although I usually put off that sort of thing, I called the producer at the TV station, ZDF, the very next morning. Looking back on it, I’m really amazed that I was so determined when I still didn’t know anything.

BOOK REVIEW: You had a nose for the romantic story.

WOLF HAAS: I can’t explain it any other way. The call to ZDF was, of course, preposterous.

BOOK REVIEW: A lot of people probably call in.

WOLF HAAS: They were actually pretty friendly, but of course they didn’t give out his address.

BOOK REVIEW: Sure. That’s confidential information.

WOLF HAAS: They did offer to give the winning contestant Kowalski my telephone number, though. Actually, it was the very same evening he won. Maybe they even ended up emailing the number to him or something. After all, I was incredibly charming on the phone.

BOOK REVIEW: But he didn’t call you back?

WOLF HAAS: Strangely enough, after I called the producer, it hit me.

BOOK REVIEW: You looked in the phonebook.

WOLF HAAS: You got it. These days everything's much easier. Before, you had to go to the main post office in Vienna and ask some bonehead employee to find you the phonebook for the Ruhr. Or you called the operator and waited on hold forever. But my other problem was that I didn't remember exactly what city in the Ruhr he came from. Was it Dortmund or Bochum or Gelsenkirchen? You have to remember that as an Austrian, everything sounds the same to me – for us everything just falls into the Ruhr "pot."

BOOK REVIEW: It's the same for us Germans, actually.

WOLF HAAS: People usually know the names because of the soccer teams.

BOOK REVIEW: You're a soccer fan?

WOLF HAAS: Not in the least, really. But because Riemer was such a fan of Schalke '04, I got into it a little bit too.

BOOK REVIEW: Riemer, you mean Kowalski's friend and co-worker, the one you met first.

WOLF HAAS: Right. So, to finish the story quickly, I just typed the name into the online telephone directory. In Austria the web address is www.etb.at – etb stands for electronic telephone book.

BOOK REVIEW: And what does "at" mean?

WOLF HAAS: Austria.

BOOK REVIEW: Oh, right. That was stupid.

WOLF HAAS: It was the same with me. I'd never searched in Germany before. Etb doesn't exist there, so on a whim I type in www.telefonbuch.de and –

BOOK REVIEW: Bingo!

WOLF HAAS: There's tons of Kowalskis in the Ruhr.

BOOK REVIEW: Right. Descendants of Polish miners. Everybody there is either a Schimanski or a Kowalski.

WOLF HAAS: It was lucky that he had such an unusual first name.

BOOK REVIEW: His first name doesn't come up in the book at all. Because he's the narrator.

WOLF HAAS: Thank God! I would have had trouble with a German named Vittorio. For one thing, it sounds really lame. And second, everything would have fit together too well.

BOOK REVIEW: Because Anni has an Italian last name.

WOLF HAAS: Yes, Bonati. Where we are there are a lot of Italian last names, especially in the Western part of Austria. But what I didn't know at the time was that you also find them all over the Ruhr because there weren't only Polish miners – there were Italians too.

BOOK REVIEW: But that doesn't explain an Italian first name. I've got to say, having a Vittorio in the novel would have been too much for me.

WOLF HAAS: Well, it's because his mother had had an Italian surname before she got married. But I always forget her maiden name.

BOOK REVIEW: You write that she always felt that she was a little bit better, with her Italian name, compared to her husband's "Kowalski," and that there was a kind of rivalry between them. She also says once to Mrs. Bonati that she envied her last name.

WOLF HAAS: In any case, she changed her Italian name when she got married, and her son had to bear the burden.

BOOK REVIEW: Well, I actually think Vittorio's really a very nice name.

WOLF HAAS: It helped me a lot. A few seconds after I typed in the name, I had his number and address up on the screen and it wasn't Bochum, Dortmund, or Gelsenkirchen. It was Essen Kupferdreh. I didn't even think of Essen.

BOOK REVIEW: Yeah, well. They don't have a good soccer team.

WOLF HAAS: Isn't there something like "Red-White Essen"?

BOOK REVIEW: Don't ask me. But I think they're still just a local club.

WOLF HAAS: Anyway, so I call him and of course I get a machine. But it was definitely his voice. He has a unique voice. I find that a person's voice says a lot about his character – sometimes even more than his words.

BOOK REVIEW: I don't recall whether the bit about his distinctive voice really came across in the book.

WOLF HAAS: No, it doesn't come up. It wouldn't work, because he's telling his own story.

BOOK REVIEW: Right. Of course, he wouldn't reflect on his own voice.

WOLF HAAS: But maybe I would have left it out anyway. I think it's really difficult to describe voices. You can characterize really extreme ones with words: shrill, resonant, etc. That's why people in novels always have shrill or booming, or nasal, or other distinctive voices – because there are words to describe them.

BOOK REVIEW: Falsetto voices?

WOLF HAAS: Exactly. But Mr. Kowalski has an absolutely average voice range. It would be difficult to find words to describe it. The characteristic thing is his tone, not his voice. The tone is somehow –

BOOK REVIEW: Constricted?

WOLF HAAS: I wouldn't put it so harshly.

BOOK REVIEW: Inhibited?

WOLF HAAS: Unreal, somehow. Contradictory. I'm happy that I didn't have to convey it in the book. An author can really tear his hair out over something like that.

BOOK REVIEW: Of course, the book itself already has a certain tone. The contradiction comes through loud and clear. For me it had an almost childlike seriousness.

WOLF HAAS: That goes well with the way he spoke on his answering machine. As if he'd dressed up in his Sunday best, combed his hair, and then recorded it. "This is the automated answering machine of Vittorio Kowalski. Unfortunately I cannot answer your call personally. If you would leave me your number I would be pleased to return your call."

BOOK REVIEW: You know it by heart.

WOLF HAAS: I called back pretty often. After two weeks, though, I realized that it wasn't getting me anywhere, so I took my chances and drove up.

BOOK REVIEW: Drove *up*? From Austria to the Ruhr, you drive *down*.

WOLF HAAS: For us it's more about the map. We drive up to the North even when it is downwards.

BOOK REVIEW: Ok, so you drove up to Essen.

WOLF HAAS: I'd never made such a long car trip in one day. At least I can write it off on my taxes, though. For that reason I'm glad the main character in my book comes from such a far-flung place.

BOOK REVIEW: Long car trips have also played an important role in Vittorio Kowalski's life and love. Why are you laughing? Is "life and love" over the top?

WOLF HAAS: Sorry. I'm not laughing at you. You just reminded me of that old triple-jackpot lottery slogan,

"Life, Love, Loss."

BOOK REVIEW: That fits too. He didn't actually lose anything, but he did suffer quite a bit on long highway drives when he was a kid.

WOLF HAAS: But I didn't know that yet. The drive was pretty tolerable for me. Anyway, I had to listen to the corrections of my latest book on tape and I like doing that in the car. Long drives were a horror for him as a child, though.

BOOK REVIEW: I think these are the strongest passages in your novel, these agonizingly long holiday drives. And how time expands for a kid so much more endlessly and tortuously than for an adult.

WOLF HAAS: I still remember his descriptions clearly. How he was carted off to vacation summer after summer, the car stuffed to the gills. And somewhere in the backseat between coolers and knapsacks and camping gear, there was a little boy counting the kilometers.

BOOK REVIEW: It's really awful reading that. I have to say it brings back memories.

WOLF HAAS: Did you do that too? Count the kilometers?

BOOK REVIEW: Not the counting. But the anxiety, the endlessly long holiday drives to the South. I remember those well. And the parents arguing in the front seat, exactly the way you describe the Kowalskis. The view of the backs of their heads and their sweaty necks. I believe that's the collective trauma of a whole generation, but counting down the kilometers like Vittorio, I didn't do that. Well, in any case, not as obsessively. I was more likely to escape into dream worlds.

WOLF HAAS: Every kid develops his own survival strategy. For him it was the counting. Converting kilometers into hours and minutes. Over the years, his calculations got so good that when they reached the longitude of Frankfurt, he could predict their arrival time in Farmach within ten minutes.

BOOK REVIEW: Just like airplanes today, where the computer screen shows you there are 5 hours and 47 minutes left before arrival at JFK.

WOLF HAAS: I find that very appealing. Basically, there's nothing more boring than vacation trips like that, so that would be anything but ideal for the beginning of a novel. And the constant countdown gives you this feeling that something is about to happen. But nothing ever does! (*laughs*)

BOOK REVIEW: You almost get the impression that he starts to hallucinate in the heat and the excruciating boredom.

WOLF HAAS: What do you mean now?

BOOK REVIEW: For instance, the air mattress in the back seat.

WOLF HAAS: I've gotten some criticism about that part with the air mattress, that it seems a bit forced.

BOOK REVIEW: One critic even made the pun that you'd over-inflated the metaphor.

WOLF HAAS: Yes, ha ha. The point is, it's no metaphor.

BOOK REVIEW: I sort of had the impression while I was reading that this isn't the same Mr. Kowalski talking, not the one who had been narrating so earnestly and seriously up until this point. The way the family drives "down" the same route year after year. Always the same landmarks. There you're really suffering along with the kid. In the extreme heat! But maybe that part with the air mattress is a little too much.

WOLF HAAS: That's the point. It was too much for him, too!

BOOK REVIEW: But when you're reading, you get the feeling that the author is interfering and trying to use particularly elaborate imagery to explain how tight and agonizing it was for the boy in the back seat. In those first years he was still quite small, and the consciousness seems somehow too sophisticated for a little kid.

WOLF HAAS: Yes, and you see, this is pretty much the only passage that I took word for word from his stories. What I really liked was how very bitterly, after so many years, he could still tick off every piece of luggage he had to share the space with in his father's different cars. So, right at the beginning it was still an old VW Beetle, and then they upgraded in the normal way: Opel Cadet, VW Golf, and so on.

BOOK REVIEW: You didn't mention the makes of the cars.

WOLF HAAS: I toyed with that idea a lot. There were,

of course, drafts where I left all of that in. Then I crossed out. I wanted to avoid making this into a kind of fashionable archaeological history of brands. I don't like this tendency of young people to look back on their little "back thens" as thirty year olds and say, "Can you even remember what was in style back then?" That's pretty ridiculous. Anyway, where was I?

BOOK REVIEW: Air mattress.

WOLF HAAS: Yes, the air mattress passage. He told me that his rolled-up air mattress had its own place in the car, right beside his legs, crammed behind the passenger seat. I was surprised to see that when he spoke about it he made a face that looked as if he were about to cry, but that was just of the his anticipatory facial expression before he started complaining about the foul rubber smell of the air mattress. Back then they didn't have any air conditioning in the car. Now I'm saying "back then" too. See, that's what I didn't want in the book, this retro-kitsch, this eternal "back then."

BOOK REVIEW: No air-conditioning isn't necessarily retro-kitsch.

WOLF HAAS: Air conditioners in general have been a theme for me. When I was a copywriter for Mazda I wrote a lot about air conditioners. It's sort of my thing. "Air-conditioning included" was the biggest hit back then.

BOOK REVIEW: Back then!

WOLF HAAS: *Yes*, terrible. Now I'm doing it too. In any case, it was because of the heat in the car that the air mattress almost melted -

BOOK REVIEW: I can well imagine that the boy suffered from the rubber smell. But “foul stench of rubber?”

WOLF HAAS: Those were his words! Foul stench of rubber! And this reserved Mr. Kowalski, he isn’t the kind of guy who searches for big words. He doesn’t say “foul” when he means “a little unpleasant.” He really must have suffered. I can imagine that this rubber thing in the prison cell of a roasting car would give off fumes that weren’t exactly non-toxic.

BOOK REVIEW: Of course the air mattress itself is also a piece of equipment that conjures up an entire world.

WOLF HAAS: Yes, true. It’s a dangerous thing. I constantly had to delete things and restrain myself. I was surprised at how obtrusive things really are. And at the incredible contrast between what a pumped-up air mattress means at a lake – so marvelous, the paddling, the sun, the water, the fresh air – and what happens to it when it suffocates someone in a hot, stinking car.

BOOK REVIEW: In certain passages it’s almost like glue-sniffing.

WOLF HAAS: Exactly! And then he also says that as a child he always imagined that the air mattress in the car was just using the air that had been allotted to its inflation to make that smell. Well, he said it better. In his version it really sounded as though the air mattress were a sick life form, a perishing organism unable to expand. The air mattress needs all the air it can get to survive its crisis there behind the passenger seat.

BOOK REVIEW: Behind the passenger seat. You also emphasize that in the book. The mother always sat in the passenger seat.

WOLF HAAS: Yes. She couldn't drive. I was always surprised by that, because otherwise she was a very modern woman.

BOOK REVIEW: Probably because of her asthma!

WOLF HAAS: (*laughs*)

BOOK REVIEW: On the other hand, his father was quite a bit older.

WOLF HAAS: He was already pushing forty when Vittorio was born.

BOOK REVIEW: But I wanted to say something about how the rolled-up air mattress was always stuck behind the passenger seat. Why do you emphasize that in the book?

WOLF HAAS: Well, that's the way he told it to me. Because his mother was bigger than his father. I found that an interesting detail somehow. The father's ancestors were miners, mine inspectors; they had to have been small. The mother was younger and taller.

BOOK REVIEW: Although she was from a line of Italians.

WOLF HAAS: Yes, odd. But she wasn't a giantess or anything. Just big enough that the son had more space behind the driver's seat. And for this reason the spot for the air mattress was behind the passenger seat. I don't think I emphasize it that much. But why are you emphasizing that I emphasize it?

BOOK REVIEW: I'm not emphasizing it. I just wonder how much the phallic symbolism of the air mattress –

WOLF HAAS: Excuse me?

BOOK REVIEW: It sort of forces itself on you. The air mattress is suffering because it isn't allowed to expand to its full size, because it is jammed behind the mother's seat.

WOLF HAAS: You won't believe it. Even in my dreams I never would – but, well, there it is.

BOOK REVIEW: Yes?

WOLF HAAS: For me I guess air mattresses are sort of lewd contraptions.

BOOK REVIEW: Well, that isn't quite the strongest counter-argument, now is it?

WOLF HAAS: No, I just mean, I think air mattresses can somehow be sensual witnesses to a time or a place, without completely falling into this back-when-we-still-drank-Tab sentimentality. Also, because the material has gone through such an interesting development over the years, from real rubber air mattresses to these ever thinner, transparent high tech skins. But mostly I just thought that you really feel how much the child suffers during the drive. Trapped in that numbing stench. And in the Beetle the gas tank was in front, which brought the gas fumes into the car, and let them build up in back around the child, like storm clouds gathering around a mountain. They build up under the rear window.

BOOK REVIEW: Yes, a lot of things build up around kids.

WOLF HAAS: I just thought the contrast was nice. That all you want to do is drive off for a vacation! Away! Into nature! Paddle far out on the lake on the air mattress.

BOOK REVIEW: You are constantly quoting the mother, who calls out at every opportunity during the vacation, "Oh, this fresh air!'

WOLF HAAS: She was always parading her asthma.

BOOK REVIEW: At the beginning I wasn't sure if that was perhaps just a stylistic technique to emphasize the contrast between the filthy air in the Ruhr and the fresh air in the mountains.

WOLF HAAS: No, no. "This fresh air," that is authentic Mrs. Kowalski. She was generally very … how should I say it? She was a windbag.

BOOK REVIEW: But my interpretation is too psychoanalytical for you.

WOLF HAAS: No, not at all. Somehow I even like it, if it weren't about my book.

BOOK REVIEW: For me that was unequivocal as I read. I thought, now here Wolf Haas is telegraphing his meaning. He sends the boy off on a trip to his first sexual experiences, and on the way he contemplates the air mattress, which isn't allowed to expand, and up front, his mother shoves her seat so far back that the air mattress is squashed.

WOLF HAAS: Oh God. I fold. It sounds to me as if you would say: air mattress, there must also be a connection with the passage where Anni's father says that Vittorio's mother looks like the town mattress.

BOOK REVIEW: Yes, because of her dyed red hair. When I read it the second time, I realized what explosive power this insult has in light of the later developments.

WOLF HAAS: There it's more about the cultural differences. It's about a particular advantage of the German summer tourists vis-à-vis the locals. Well, in those days there were still a lot of differences.

BOOK REVIEW: Was it more city vs. country or German vs. Austrian?

WOLF HAAS: I think both. In any case, the brassy dyed hair is a classic example. At the time there were still many differences between the local women and the female tourists with their fashionable clothes and everything. I wanted to capture how Bonati, who himself was working class, once said to his wife that Vittorio's mother looked like the town mattress with her dyed red hair.

BOOK REVIEW: But only under his breath, of course.

WOLF HAAS: It was an accident that Anni happened to overhear it, and she had to solemnly swear to her mother that she wouldn't repeat it. And that same day Vittorio had to solemnly swear that he wouldn't repeat it to his parents.

BOOK REVIEW: He was really true to his word.

WOLF HAAS: He was always true to everything.

BOOK REVIEW: But don't worry. I didn't link the Mrs. Kowalski town mattress insult to the air mattress passage.

WOLF HAAS: Then I'm really happy now that I took out some of the air mattress parts because I'd originally written a lot more about the swimming scenes. The way the children would paddle out on the air mattress. Children shoving each other, letting the air out, and all that horsing around.

BOOK REVIEW: Too bad you cut that. There's a lot of childlike eroticism in it. Maybe it would have seemed less symbolic if there'd been more skin.

WOLF HAAS: In a previous version I used the air mattress to convey the passage of time. For example, the way he had a double air mattress one day. Boy, was he proud. I found his story really funny, the way he noticed as he paddled out that the double air mattress didn't work.

BOOK REVIEW: What do you mean it didn't work?

WOLF HAAS: Well, when you lie on your stomach on an air mattress, your arms hang off into the water to the left and right. So you can paddle with them. That was a story I really liked, when Mr. Kowalski told me how proud he was of his new double mattress, but when he first tried to paddle out, he noticed that his hands couldn't reach into the water on the sides because it was too wide! (*laughs*)

BOOK REVIEW: Nothing works any more in the marriage bed.

WOLF HAAS: Right.

BOOK REVIEW: Why did you omit the passage if you liked it so much?

WOLF HAAS: Just because I thought it was too symbolic. The extra-large air mattress, the whole queen-sized bed symbolism, or no, not symbolism at all. Simply the actual possibility that you could lie side by side on it and everything. Telegraphing my meaning, as you said. And now you're saying that even the rolled-up mattress conveys this. I really like it when authors overlook things like this and, just as you try to avoid it, it appears. The highly edited passages are always the most boring, anyway.

BOOK REVIEW: It's a shame that you cut all that out. I would have liked to know more about this summer idyll where these children grew up together. You tell it very briefly. Even just the swans on the Waldsee that Anni and Vittorio used to feed with leftover breakfast rolls.

WOLF HAAS: Yes, that gets kitschy pretty fast. But you can also exaggerate it by cutting it. There was one version where I had even cut out the part about that truck inner tube.

BOOK REVIEW: Anni's swimming tube? That would have been a shame. I have to say, that was one of the most impressive passages in the book – where the reader feels she's right there. It's as if you'd experienced it yourself. As if you yourself had swum out into the

Waldsee with this black truck tire for a tube.

WOLF HAAS: Yes. Actually it wasn't really a swimming tube in that sense. Well, so long as she couldn't swim it would have been too dangerous as a float for a non-swimmer. And anyway, a truck inner tube is much too big for that. A little girl would slide right through it. And Anni was always a string bean.

BOOK REVIEW: You stress that more than once, that Anni was a string bean. This expression got to you.

WOLF HAAS: That's only because her father always called her that, a little string bean. I think she liked it because she herself told it to me a few times.

BOOK REVIEW: Also she couldn't pronounce it as a child.

WOLF HAAS: Yes, exactly. Stwingbean.

BOOK REVIEW: That's much more natural. Stwing-bean.

WOLF HAAS: I think so too.

BOOK REVIEW: In any case, the truck tire inner tube would have been too big for her.

WOLF HAAS: Much too big! For flotation, she used a normal-sized car inner tube. When she was really little, it was a motorbike inner tube. Small, but just as black. Not a colorful kiddie toy.

BOOK REVIEW: You automatically imagine the air

mattress to be yellow and blue, although you don't give away the color in the book. As the author, did you have anything to do with the cover design?

WOLF HAAS: No. But I think the cover is really great. Today most book covers are as loud as jogging suits. So I was really lucky there.

BOOK REVIEW: Air mattresses are also much brighter these days.

WOLF HAAS: Naturally, Vittorio also switched over to these as time went by. He had a new one almost every year, but Anni's tubes were always black. As constant in their fashion as the suits of priests and architects. And wet rubber looks particularly black!

BOOK REVIEW: I notice that you said before that memories of childhood summers are too kitschy for you. Apparently you could tolerate the black inner tube better than a colorful swimming tube or even little water wings.

WOLF HAAS: Well, that's just the way it was because Anni's father was a truck driver. So, he gave her this truck tire tube. It wasn't a flotation device anymore – it was her boat! When I was a kid, I used to see that kind of thing a lot. Where I come from it was usually farmers' children who had tractor inner tubes. They were incredible giants. Sea monsters. Or even inner tubes from backhoe tires. Huge backhoe tire tubes. With their store-bought water wings and air mattresses, Toys 'R' Us kids just can't compete.

BOOK REVIEW: Like Vittorio.

WOLF HAAS: And in Anni's case, it was something special because she got the tube from her father. From the paternal truck. A gigantic thing, to carry the princess across the lake.

BOOK REVIEW: That reminded me of an illustration in a children's book. The way little Thumbelina sails across the lake on a linden leaf.

WOLF HAAS: Yes, something like that. It was enormous. A huge hunk of rubber from the Bonati-mobile. It's only dangerous if you scrape your stomach on the valve.

BOOK REVIEW: I was just thinking that. Well, I'm wondering if I should question my perceptions. Maybe it was right to skim over the summer idyll after all. I can confirm that even after these few scenes the reader is convinced that Vittorio and Anni somehow belong together. That they are happy when they are together and not so happy when they are apart.

WOLF HAAS: That much is clear.

BOOK REVIEW: And you really can't accept that he suddenly stops going to see her in the summer and that for fifteen years he doesn't travel to her village and doesn't have any contact with her at all.

WOLF HAAS: That is painful. It's really a brutal story. And everything was just because of a stupid stroke of bad luck.

BOOK REVIEW: Such a waste.

WOLF HAAS: But after fifteen years he does drive

down again.

BOOK REVIEW: Otherwise we wouldn't be sitting here talking about it.

WOLF HAAS: Right. Otherwise it wouldn't be a movie – as my Aunt Sefa used to say when she watched TV when we were making fun of some cheesy film.

BOOK REVIEW: Otherwise it wouldn't be a movie. Right. If Vittorio hadn't received the postcard from his old vacation spot two weeks after his appearance on *Place Your Bets* and driven down the very same day.

WOLF HAAS: For me, that was hard to take at first, that I'd missed him by just one day. I think we might even have passed each other on the highway. And when was standing there at his door, he was arriving in Farmach for the first time in fifteen years.

BOOK REVIEW: We'll speak about that tomorrow, Mr. Haas.

Day Two

BOOK REVIEW: Mr. Haas, your long drive from Vienna to the Ruhr turned out to be pretty disappointing.

WOLF HAAS: Naturally I was disappointed at first that I didn't meet with Kowalski, but in hindsight you have to say that for the story it was the best thing I could have hoped for.

BOOK REVIEW: Because at the same time that you were driving up he was traveling in the opposite direction.

WOLF HAAS: Anni's postcard with the mountain panorama that he found in his mailbox two weeks after the TV show was, of course, more interesting than my phone messages.

BOOK REVIEW: The postcard, which was actually from his friend Riemer.

WOLF HAAS: Yeah, Riemer played God a little bit there. He felt sorry for his friend. He never could have predicted the chain of events he set in motion.

BOOK REVIEW: I can already see that we have to, at least briefly, talk about your experience in the Ruhr. You mentioned that the Ruhr would have been a novel in and of itself.

WOLF HAAS: Oh, I just said that. It's true that while I was working on it, for a while I would have found it fun to move the whole second part of the story, the part set in the present, to the Ruhr – so that after the TV show, Anni would drive to see him instead of his driving to see her. That was impossible, of course. That would have been a completely different book, but the appeal lay in the symmetry. That you'd have a sort of pendulum swing.

BOOK REVIEW: For fifteen years one of them drives down, now she drives up.

WOLF HAAS: Also because there are always these places people drive to. You always travel from England to Spain, always from Munich to Venice, always from the Ruhr to Austria and never the other way. Naturally it would have been appealing to write it the other way around for once. An Austrian tourist in the Ruhr, as it were. But I couldn't do that. To this day she hasn't been up north.

BOOK REVIEW: What? That's unbelievable. After this whole story?

WOLF HAAS: Yes, she's not very sentimental.

BOOK REVIEW: That sounds kind of cold, somehow. After all their whole history!

WOLF HAAS: But looking back on it I'm also glad that I couldn't turn it around. After all, I think that for the purposes of the book, having one defined direction is more dynamic than multiple compass points. I always say that artifice begins with symmetry. But instead, everything goes in one direction – down, down, down. Just like real life!

BOOK REVIEW: You, on the other hand, drove up.

WOLF HAAS: Yes. And it was really exciting for me.

BOOK REVIEW: How did you search for him, anyway?

WOLF HAAS: Back in Vienna I found out where he worked. These days Google makes everything eerily simple.

BOOK REVIEW: You bet I did it before our meeting too. About you, I know –

WOLF HAAS: Everything.

BOOK REVIEW: I wouldn't say "everything," but you can find out a lot.

WOLF HAAS: I found out a lot about you, too.

BOOK REVIEW: What? Really? But there isn't anything!

WOLF HAAS: There's a lot, in fact. Marathon results, for instance.

BOOK REVIEW: Oh God. That was just a fun run.

WOLF HAAS: But with Mr. Kowalski, it was pure luck that there happened to be something about his work on Google. He didn't have anything to do with public relations – he and his friend Riemer divided up the work pretty strictly. Kowalski was responsible for the "real work" – for the dry technical stuff. When there was something to calculate and prove or document, he took care of it. Riemer's been working the past few years in public relations.

BOOK REVIEW: You found out more about Riemer on the internet.

WOLF HAAS: I still had no idea of Riemer's existence. I could have found hundreds of articles on him. There is always something in the local papers about his opposition to the so-called "'Groundless' Citizens' Initiative." I found all that later. Before I drove up I had no idea at all about the whole problem with the abandoned mine shafts. You don't hear a lot about it back home, but in the Ruhr newspapers you read about it constantly.

BOOK REVIEW: About the fear that when people are taking a walk they could be swallowed up by an inadequately filled-in mine shaft – become "groundless."

WOLF HAAS: But in Austria that's not a huge topic, of course.

BOOK REVIEW: Although interestingly enough something like that did happen in Austria a few years ago! It was on the news, that the houses in this mining community sank right into the ground. Lassnig?

WOLF HAAS: Lassing. Lassnig is a painter.

BOOK REVIEW: Lassing.

WOLF HAAS: But of course you can't begin to compare the two on the same scale. That was just a couple of houses that sank. When I think about the outrage that erupted in our country after that accident, it's easy to extrapolate the potential threat for unrest in the Ruhr. I estimate that the Ruhr has maybe as many inhabitants as all of Austria. If they were to be swallowed up, that would be really something.

BOOK REVIEW: So when you drove up you actually

knew that Mr. Kowalski worked at IMR?

WOLF HAAS: Yes, Infrastructure Management Ruhr. I knew that from Gottschalk's TV show. He mentioned it there and even made a joke he'd practiced. It fell flat. He said he was in the demolition business – more specifically that he tore down old mines.

BOOK REVIEW: Well, the joke came across better in the book. I laughed.

WOLF HAAS: The author helped a little.

BOOK REVIEW: Yes, well. That's your job. Let's say, that suggests that you already had a pretty clear idea of his daily life when you drove up.

WOLF HAAS: Not really. Mine-demolition, that didn't mean a lot to me. I also have to admit that I had an anachronistic idea of the Ruhr. Some of it was just due to the fact that, as an Austrian, one has nothing to do with that part of the world.

BOOK REVIEW: You thought that white laundry hung out on the line to dry in the morning was black by evening.

WOLF HAAS: Well, of course I knew the mines there are more or less out of commission, but when there is no real contact, the old images are even more persistent. Such a suggestive word as "Ruhr" conjures a certain image and somehow it was indeed – against my better judgment – still a vision of coal and soot. A kind of world of headlamps and buddies came to mind when I heard the word "Ruhr." Or Ruhr "pot" or "coal fields." In the meantime, I found out the locals don't necessarily use these terms.

BOOK REVIEW: The way no one in San Francisco calls the place Frisco.

WOLF HAAS: Something like that. Or, for instance, I can't yodel.

BOOK REVIEW: You don't say.

WOLF HAAS: By that, I only mean that when you're looking at something from far off you have to be careful not to cling to the dumb clichés and simplifications. I was even tempted to turn it into a theme in the book, the whole underground world. The mine ventilation thing, the seals on the mine shafts, the mine inspectors. Well, Vittorio's ancestors were mine inspectors for generations. For me, as an Austrian, all this sounds somehow interesting and exotic. Of course it has nothing to do with Vittorio Kowalski's passion for the weather in his childhood vacation spot.

BOOK REVIEW: How was it for you when you arrived?

WOLF HAAS: It had nothing to do with negative romanticism. Highway and drizzle. That's my main memory.

BOOK REVIEW: Instead, your positive romantic expectations for the love story were met.

WOLF HAAS: Yes, even exceeded, you have to admit.

BOOK REVIEW: Even though you never met up with Kowalski.

WOLF HAAS: That was a total flop. I was just lucky that the expression "you snooze, you lose" isn't always true. In my case, it was actually a huge plus because his friend Riemer is such an extrovert. This friendly guy was a real godsend.

BOOK REVIEW: I must say, I didn't find Riemer terribly appealing.

WOLF HAAS: I can understand that, but, of course, he was the jackpot for me. I wouldn't have found out half so much from Kowalski himself. It's difficult to imagine two more different guys. Naturally Riemer is – I take it this is what you mean – an obnoxious womanizer.

BOOK REVIEW: He's a philanderer. That's how it comes across in the book. What, with his *Women for Dummies* course at night school and everything. Does that course really exist?

WOLF HAAS: Sure. But *Women for Dummies* was earlier. I just mentioned it because Riemer once tried to persuade Kowalski to take the course. He suspected his friend had never been involved with a woman.

BOOK REVIEW: Didn't Riemer know anything about Anni?

WOLF HAAS: Next to nothing. Riemer just got the impression through his day-to-day contact with Kowalski that something wasn't right in that department. That's why he was so desperate to drag him to *Women for Dummies*. He himself was far beyond that stage. He had already been signed up for the Italian course for years.

BOOK REVIEW: Because of the surplus of women.

WOLF HAAS: He actually learned from *Women for Dummies*, that men always look in the wrong places when they want to meet women. That, for example, many more attractive women are sitting in any given Italian course than in a sports bar or a Bruce Willis movie.

BOOK REVIEW: The way I see Riemer, he's mighty proud of his role in your book.

WOLF HAAS: Just last week he called to say that the book had helped him achieve new levels of female devotion. Don't laugh. He calls them the "intellectuals!"

BOOK REVIEW: Because they've read your book.

WOLF HAAS: Exactly.

BOOK REVIEW: One can only hope that he managed to achieve his longed-for Silver Star Orgasm. It never occurred to you to omit that?

WOLF HAAS: I just thought his ambition was hilarious. And also that the two friends complemented each other in the level of their devotion. One is exclusively interested in the weather in a distant village, and the other's only concern is –

BOOK REVIEW: – the Silver Star Orgasm.

WOLF HAAS: Well, I wouldn't reduce it to that, now. The expression does have a function in the book! Riemer once read somewhere in a magazine about this paradox:

that you remember particularly intense emotional experiences poorly in retrospect. That made him very uneasy.

BOOK REVIEW: Because he can still remember his Saturday night adventures so well.

WOLF HAAS: He would immediately report everything to Kowalski at the office on Monday morning.

BOOK REVIEW: And he sometimes liked to give the women scores.

WOLF HAAS: Not the women! Just the experiences. Well, the erotic intensity, I think. To put it bluntly, he graded the sex.

BOOK REVIEW: Very nice! I really must say.

WOLF HAAS: He was even afraid that there could be an intensity he wasn't even aware of. A world to which he had no access. This made him think back to his elementary school teacher who would sometimes skip the traditional grading system entirely and give not only an A, but also paste a little silver star in your notebook.

BOOK REVIEW: Hmm.

WOLF HAAS: Yes, well. I saw the funny side of it. Of course it is a bit obsessive.

BOOK REVIEW: Okay, but this isn't about Riemer, but rather the information he gave you about his friend who had spontaneously taken off for Austria. Except that, in night school, rather than taking the *Women for Dummies* course that Riemer recommended, for years he'd been taking a course on how to stop oneself from blushing.

WOLF HAAS: My primary interest was how he came to appear on *Place Your Bets*.

BOOK REVIEW: In the novel it seems that Riemer initiated the challenge.

WOLF HAAS: Riemer told me the actual instigator was Claudia the secretary. She was the one who gave Riemer the idea. Naturally, Claudia never would have dared to sign her boss up at ZDF on her own, so she pulled some strings with Riemer.

BOOK REVIEW: Yes, that's the way you tell it in the book. Claudia the secretary doesn't play a central role at all. At first you have the impression while reading that Riemer is the main character in the novel. You think Kowalski is telling the story of his friend. Did you intend this impression?

WOLF HAAS: I admit I didn't necessarily have a choice there. A guy like Riemer can go wherever he wants and give the impression that he is the main character.

BOOK REVIEW: You're arguing that a real character would have left you no choice? That brings up a few pointed analogies to your earlier work in the sense that you distance yourself from naïve realism, a style that characterizes most thrillers.

WOLF HAAS: I only said that at the time because I was too lazy to do research.

BOOK REVIEW: Oh, no.

WOLF HAAS: I think it's much easier to invent a story. You don't have to talk with anyone. That's why I made such a big deal out of my phone call to ZDF yesterday. Sure, I was a little embarrassed afterwards about having made such a fuss, but for me there's something exciting about it, making a call like that. And then, I just drove up!

BOOK REVIEW: That almost sounds like behavioral therapy.

WOLF HAAS: Yes. Then I would have earned a silver star, too. And the next day I looked up Riemer in his office.

BOOK REVIEW: Mr. Haas: A Journey into Reality.

WOLF HAAS: But I didn't know it then. At the beginning I still believed that I was just going to collect a little material and that maybe I could make something out of Riemer's stories.

BOOK REVIEW: And how did Riemer react to your showing up?

WOLF HAAS: He was very nice! The people in the Ruhr are very nice in general. We should send all the bastards in our tourism industry up there for training so they can see how normal people behave. He even took me to his favorite pub that same day.

BOOK REVIEW: And he told you everything immediately?

WOLF HAAS: No, not quite. We went there several evenings in a row and stood at the bar. Along the way he turned up the heat for a couple of ladies.

BOOK REVIEW: Turned up the heat?

WOLF HAAS: Yes, I mean came on to them. Flirted. Where I come from, we say turned up the heat.

BOOK REVIEW: Oh, that's mouth-watering. Actually, you showed up right on cue while his friend Kowalski was away. Guys like that always need a buddy for their heating rituals.

WOLF HAAS: Maybe that was also a factor. The whole time he described his friend very empathetically. I must say that because you don't have a lot of trust in such a space cadet.

BOOK REVIEW: I have to say the only redeeming thing about Riemer is that, of all people, he sought out this strange Mr. Kowalski as a friend.

WOLF HAAS: I believe you're judging Riemer a little harshly. Anyway, you have to say that without Riemer there never would have been a reunion with Anni. Again, he was also very sensitive to that. Kowalski had barely told him anything about Anni. Well, at most only marginally, that as a child he always went back to the same village in Austria on vacation and always stayed in the same bed and breakfast. Maybe the daughter of the landlord came up a couple of times, but that was about it.

BOOK REVIEW: But Riemer put the pieces together.

WOLF HAAS: Yes! It took someone as obsessive as Riemer. He just didn't believe that his shy friend was just simply interested in the weather in his childhood vacation spot. It was clear to him that there had to be a woman behind it.

BOOK REVIEW: Although he wasn't at all aware that his friend knew the weather by heart only starting from a certain day. The day he saw Anni for the last time.

WOLF HAAS: Yes, you have to hand it to Riemer. He's got great antennae for that sort of thing.

BOOK REVIEW: He probably learned that in the course too. *Women for Dummies*, Advanced Level. Women fall for sensitive men.

WOLF HAAS: I can see that you just don't like him.

BOOK REVIEW: Yes, well. It's not really a question of whether I like him or not. You can at least say that Riemer isn't entirely unselfish. Kowalski was sort of an ideal Saturday night sidekick.

WOLF HAAS: That's true. With two people it's easier to start a conversation. And in conversations about the weather, Kowalski was always the ice breaker.

BOOK REVIEW: In the book you write "can opener" not "ice breaker."

WOLF HAAS: Yes, well, the shoehorn, if you like. He was just good at giving women original answers to off-hand weather observations. So, when someone would say "the weather is really oppressive today" or something like that, he could say something about it. And not the usual male bullshit, like, whatever.

BOOK REVIEW: I wouldn't mind showing you some high pressure.

WOLF HAAS: Exactly. Instead it was just something meteorological. Naturally it was good for Riemer that his friend always disappeared at just the right moment. Otherwise you just end up getting in each other's way.

BOOK REVIEW: Vittorio always had to call up Mrs. Bachl before midnight to get the weather report.

WOLF HAAS: Yes. He'd figured out that he wouldn't sleep well if he hadn't first called Anni's old neighbor to find out the current weather conditions in Farmach. Even though Mrs. Bachl always insisted that it wouldn't be a problem if he called after midnight. She was already so old that she didn't sleep anymore anyway. But midnight was the limit for him. He only called later once or twice, in extreme emergencies.

BOOK REVIEW: I'd like to devote some time to Mrs. Bachl. She's my favorite character.

WOLF HAAS: Really? Mine too! Although she barely appears in the novel.

BOOK REVIEW: I need more time for Mrs. Bachl. The way she always sits there on her red bench under the flower trellis and looks up smiling at the sky. And her dentures reflect the sunset!

WOLF HAAS: Anni's father always said "Bachl's been sitting there on her red bench watching the weather since the world was created."

BOOK REVIEW: Yes, you really get that impression

while reading. But let's stay with the advantages that Riemer enjoyed through his acquaintance with Kowalski.

WOLF HAAS: All women like to talk about the weather.

BOOK REVIEW: Oh, now that's another statement I would have expected from Riemer.

WOLF HAAS: Or most women. Many women.

BOOK REVIEW: But the real Promised Land opened up for the creep after the appearance on *Place Your Bets.*

WOLF HAAS: After that show, Mr. Kowalski couldn't go two steps without someone approaching him. Like a rock star! Naturally Riemer milked this for all it was worth.

BOOK REVIEW: But this new popularity also led to conflict between the two.

WOLF HAAS: Riemer got mad because after the show Kowalski became more distant day by day. But that's not so hard to understand. In the week after the show, he was veritably stormed by his fans –

BOOK REVIEW: – female fans, for the most part –

WOLF HAAS: – so he got to be pretty aloof. Which was utterly unlike him. He is actually a very friendly person, and Riemer just didn't understand how his friend could become so grouchy.

BOOK REVIEW: Mr. Kowalski was more a representative of the "Down with Women!" school of thought.

WOLF HAAS: Not at all! He was just annoyed that they all asked him the same question.

BOOK REVIEW: "So, how's the weather looking for tomorrow?"

WOLF HAAS: Yes, that's pretty tough to take. According to Riemer, the polite Mr. Kowalski flipped out. This was the time when he first coined the pejorative concept, "average weather consumer."

BOOK REVIEW: It occurred to me that this average weather consumer is mentioned in almost every interview about the book. You seem to have hit a nerve there.

WOLF HAAS: Somehow I can understand his frustration, though. If you make your name from such a nice quiz show challenge – and you're the only person who pays attention to the weather of the past, instead of the future – then people are going to stop you on the street and ask you this stupid question.

BOOK REVIEW: "So, how's the weather looking for tomorrow?"

WOLF HAAS: Yes, it's really a joke, isn't it?

BOOK REVIEW: In reality there was an entirely different reason for his anger. He was frustrated because all these women approached him, but not the one he cared about.

WOLF HAAS: Well, that's only partially true.

BOOK REVIEW: It must have been terribly disappointing for him that the woman he appeared *for* was the only one who didn't react.

WOLF HAAS: Now you're talking about a central point. That was the deciding question for me. I myself realized by and by that he was actually fooling himself there. He never really admitted to himself that his passion for the weather had something to do with Anni.

BOOK REVIEW: That can't possibly be true.

WOLF HAAS: It was actually Riemer who made the connection through his fixation. Kowalski himself had really forgotten about Anni in certain ways over the years. Well, not really forgotten, but –

BOOK REVIEW: – lost track of her.

WOLF HAAS: You have to be more Hegelian about it. The weather sublated Anni in the Hegelian sense.

BOOK REVIEW: Now you're really –

WOLF HAAS: In a threefold sense: temperature, air pressure, and precipitation.

BOOK REVIEW: You're really having a great time aren't you?

WOLF HAAS: With that, I'm just trying to say: consciously, he was only interested in the weather. His memories of Anni were fading more and more.

BOOK REVIEW: In your book there's the horrible sentence: "In the long run, no human being is as interesting as the weather."

WOLF HAAS: I don't think that's so horrible. Well, I think that's just a reality. Most people think they are pretty interesting, but to be honest –

BOOK REVIEW: Clearly, Mr. Kowalski didn't see it as cynically as you do. Anyway, Anni stayed interested in him for a very long time.

WOLF HAAS: The weather was really his salvation. Sooner or later that had to turn strange. He matured. When he went on the television program, he was a thirty-year-old man. He couldn't still keep on adoring a fifteen-year-old girl. It would be okay for the first few years, but eventually it would be –

BOOK REVIEW: Pedophilia.

WOLF HAAS: Well, not quite pedophilia. They were actually the same age.
The memory just had less and less to do with reality, so over time the weather came to replace the beloved.

BOOK REVIEW: So you maintain in all seriousness that in the end he didn't think about Anni at all?

WOLF HAAS: Of course, you have to ask why the weather in her village, of all places. For example, he has no idea what the weather is like in his own area. He just says that the weather in the Ruhr is generally boring.

BOOK REVIEW: Yes, but that's true though. All year they have the same soup. You can't compare that to the weather in the Alps.

WOLF HAAS: Could be. I've got to say, I'm not especially interested in the weather. I just notice that the weather's bad when my girlfriend starts acting crazy.

BOOK REVIEW: You write a book about the weather with a weather expert as your main character, but neither the author nor the protagonist is interested in the weather.

WOLF HAAS: (*laughs*) Yes, that's a problem. For me it was really tedious work until I got a handle on it. The weather vocabulary. Adriatic Lows and Biscay Highs.

BOOK REVIEW: Vice-versa.

WOLF HAAS: There, you see what I mean?

BOOK REVIEW: But I think that through your writing you could make the point that not too many people know as much as Mr. Kowalski.

WOLF HAAS: Yes, that's true, but an author can only make that point if he himself knows about it.

BOOK REVIEW: Makes sense. It isn't evident in the book that you were having difficulties. Or maybe it is, now that you mention it. Maybe you packed in just a little too much of your hard-won knowledge. Personally, I'm pretty interested in the weather, unlike Mr. Kowalski and you, but the degree of detail in the novel was sometimes a bit much for me as I read.

WOLF HAAS: It is possible to overdo something just because you're not really interested in it. That can happen to an author very easily. When you're really an expert, you feel relaxed enough to leave it out, or treat it in one or two lines.

BOOK REVIEW: Oh, so that's why the real love story is mentioned only briefly.

WOLF HAAS: Yes, ha ha. Because I'm such an expert in that.

BOOK REVIEW: Anyway, you write in greater detail about the weather than about the actual love story.

WOLF HAAS: I had to pry it out of him. His emotional life has always been extremely tied up with the weather, and that always led to so many problems!

BOOK REVIEW: At the beginning it's irritating that his love life is so tied to the weather, even with respect to Anni.

WOLF HAAS: Love life, that's a good one. Looking back on it, you almost wonder why he tried to establish any kind of regular sexual life at all. He could just as well have said, "I'm not interested in any of this. I'm only interested in the weather in my childhood vacation spot. Period."

BOOK REVIEW: Instead, he started up several real relationships with women.

WOLF HAAS: He really tried hard. The whole going to the movies, and going out to dinner and inviting them up to his apartment and candlelight and music and drinks--he went through all that. It's just that at the crucial moment, he dropped the ball.

BOOK REVIEW: And started to talk about the weather.

WOLF HAAS: And weather from way in the past, at that.

BOOK REVIEW: In Anni's village.

WOLF HAAS: And at the worst possible moment! At the beginning it was fine. In the getting to know you phase it was always an advantage. A sensitive man who can talk with you about the weather, and so on.

BOOK REVIEW: Although it didn't interest him at the level of the average weather consumer.

WOLF HAAS: He really made compromises! He exercised great self-control. In retrospect I'm amazed at how he bent over backwards.

BOOK REVIEW: He knew something wasn't quite right with him. At least according to popular opinion. In our society there's just so much pressure to be normal.

WOLF HAAS: That's why – at least, before his TV appearance – he was always ready to converse at the level of an average weather consumer, and of course he could do that better than normal men.

BOOK REVIEW: In the book Kowalski stresses that he was even ready to speak about "soft topics."

WOLF HAAS: Yes, weather-sensitivity. Weather-wellness, and the like. That was, of course, the number one topic among the female average weather consumers. He finally realized that he couldn't get around it.

Sensitivity to the weather is a really inexhaustible subject.

BOOK REVIEW: Those are terrific, the different kinds he lists. From general weather sensitivity to genuine pre-sensitivity.

WOLF HAAS: Yes, it's a great word. I think so too. I wrote the first love story with the word "pre-sensitivity."

BOOK REVIEW: No one can take that from you.

WOLF HAAS: These women, with their symptoms of fatigue, tension, sleeplessness, lack of concentration, joint pain, dizziness, scar pains, phantom pains, and shortness of breath.

BOOK REVIEW: At the risk of exposing myself as an average weather consumer, I really liked the part about the animals as weather augurs.

WOLF HAAS: A lot of people also really like the farmer's almanac rules, rhymed sayings and unrhymed, Groundhog Day, then the influence of the moon, animal augurs, swallows, spiders, bees, frogs, ants, and snails.

BOOK REVIEW: It was just the mosquitoes he was afraid of.

WOLF HAAS: The mosquitoes were naturally a dangerous topic for him because they led him in the wrong direction.

BOOK REVIEW: In the direction of the weather fifteen years ago in Anni's home town.

WOLF HAAS: Right. If the mosquitoes were already being aggressive in the afternoon instead of at sunset, a storm was on the way. Of course, for him that had a different meaning than a bunch of snails crawling up a blade of grass, or, in my opinion, ants carrying their eggs back to the nest.

BOOK REVIEW: Yes, but if it hadn't been the mosquitoes, something else would have derailed him.

WOLF HAAS: Yes, exactly. The closer a woman came to him, the greater the danger was that he would cross the line.

BOOK REVIEW: Insofar as he was a normal man.

WOLF HAAS: So then, at two or three in the morning, according to the normal rules of play, instead of the usual pawing, he would start to really talk about the weather. Not the weather tomorrow or seven day forecast, not weather sensitivity, but just –

BOOK REVIEW: – the weather fifteen years ago.

WOLF HAAS: Exactly. Maybe he'd just start with weather eight or nine years ago. He sort of worked his way up to it. It wasn't that he immediately started off with the weather fifteen years ago.

BOOK REVIEW: But just the weather in the place where he went on vacation as a child?

WOLF HAAS: Naturally that broke the mood. Or perhaps, for a while one or the other may have listened to him, captivated. An interesting man, or something. There exists this idea among certain women that there is such a thing. But at some point his advantage turned into a massive disadvantage and then he wasn't the sensitive man you could talk to about the weather anymore. Sooner or later came the dreaded sentence.

BOOK REVIEW: "Man, all you can do is talk about the weather."

WOLF HAAS: Exactly. All you can do is talk about the weather.

BOOK REVIEW: This sentence really hurts when you read it. Right in the middle of the romantic mood. All you can do is talk about the weather. You also don't spare the reader - this sentence frequently finds its way into the book.

WOLF HAAS: I'm afraid he got his face rubbed in it more than once.

BOOK REVIEW: But not all women were so brutal to him.

WOLF HAAS: I'm not talking about "brutal" at all. I really don't see things from the perspective of "it's the woman's fault," because they lack understanding or something. You can't say my book implies that.

BOOK REVIEW: Wolf Haas, the great expert on women.

WOLF HAAS: The whole discussion that was sparked by my alleged portrayal of Anni, I've got to say, I just don't care. You can infer anything you want. I think the things that have been said about me are pretty stupid. But I can understand how people drew those conclusions.

BOOK REVIEW: Because you write everything only from the man's viewpoint.

WOLF HAAS: That is the most moronic thing that anybody can say about a book. As if an author's pseudo-democratic impartiality, which pretends to understand all perspectives weren't the most blatant attempt to ingratiate oneself.

BOOK REVIEW: Fine. We can get to that later when we speak about Anni.

WOLF HAAS: In any case, I can understand those women who kick Mr. Kowalski out in the middle of the night. It's pretty insulting, when a man in that situation can't think of anything better to do than talk about the weather.

BOOK REVIEW: In the final analysis, it was just such a situation that led to his appearance on Gottschalk's TV show.

WOLF HAAS: As I said, some women reacted with more understanding and patience than he could ever have expected. Only a few got really mad. Most of them just let him talk until the right moment came to push him gently out the door.

BOOK REVIEW: But Claudia the secretary was really inspired by this passion of his!

WOLF HAAS: Yes. She was, as Riemer put it, "also a bit of a romantic."

BOOK REVIEW: Like his friend Kowalski.

WOLF HAAS: That was why Riemer wanted to set them up. Also because he saw his friend was slowly heading for a crisis. All of these experiences were beginning to leave their mark on him. All that "all you can do is talk about the weather" stuff.

BOOK REVIEW: And that made Claudia the secretary actually the first woman to react differently.

WOLF HAAS: She is just the kind of person who is more interested in romantic stories than in her own experiences.

BOOK REVIEW: A perfect match.

WOLF HAAS: Maybe, but she's twenty years younger than me.

BOOK REVIEW: No, I meant Mr. Kowalski and Claudia the secretary would have been a perfect match.

WOLF HAAS: Yes, those two! By all means! And Claudia the secretary really liked him. That's also why Riemer tried to encourage them.

BOOK REVIEW: The interesting thing about Claudia's reaction was that she didn't see his weather report as a personal insult.

WOLF HAAS: You have to give her a lot of credit for that. Maybe it helped that she knew him from work. She just knew that Mr. Kowalski was the opposite of the type who puts other people down. He is an absolutely reserved, or maybe I shouldn't use such a loaded word –

BOOK REVIEW: Is “reserved” so loaded?

WOLF HAAS: Anyway, just a quiet person. Not a bigmouth.

BOOK REVIEW: Bigmouth?

WOLF HAAS: Chatterbox.

BOOK REVIEW: He’s really the opposite of a chatterbox.

WOLF HAAS: Well, he’s also not the super silent type. Actually pretty normal.

BOOK REVIEW: As long as he doesn’t start talking about the weather fifteen years ago.

WOLF HAAS: Or about any other day in Farmach’s distant past. He only got to the actual weather fifteen years ago maybe two or three times.

BOOK REVIEW: In your book, Kowalski remembers that it was because of Claudia’s surprising interest that he first talked about the influence of the volcanoes on the weather. Is that true, or did you see it as a foreshadowing of the accident that awaited him in Farmach?

WOLF HAAS: Well. The volcanoes. You’re suddenly giving them a lot of weight. In the book, I don’t think it’s anything more than an aside.

BOOK REVIEW: It says here that Claudia the secretary was the first person with whom he could really talk about the weather.

WOLF HAAS: Really *talk weather.*

BOOK REVIEW: I stumbled over this phrase at first when I was reading. That you could really *talk weather* with her.

WOLF HAAS: It's like talking turkey. Really *talk weather.*

BOOK REVIEW: The first woman with whom he could really *talk weather.* Someone who isn't just interested in tomorrow's forecast or her sensitivity to the weather, but instead, if I can summarize, someone who cares about the details. And he lists everything he was able to tell her. It starts with some cloud changes and culminates in the sentence "the way a violent volcanic eruption lifts the cover between the troposphere and the stratosphere, presses the clouds up into the stratosphere and thus influences the weather across continents."

WOLF HAAS: Now you're putting me on the spot. I probably can't deny that there's a certain prefiguring of the accident. I'm just a little bit cautious because I don't want to test my readers' patience by making them constantly go on some Easter egg hunt for clues.

BOOK REVIEW: Of course. Otherwise the book would turn into a stupid puzzle that you'd have to solve.

WOLF HAAS: Basically, it's about the influence of the volcanoes on the weather. That's why I describe it so exactly, the way even the weather in the troposphere happens because there are no more clouds up in the stratosphere. Except when a volcano produces such a violent updraft that the lid that holds the stratosphere over the troposphere gets pushed up.

BOOK REVIEW: The tropopause.

WOLF HAAS: That should remain as straightforward and un-metaphorical as possible, but naturally when you know the end of the story you hear a certain rumbling during the conversation about the volcanoes. It wouldn't bother me if a reader were to say: aha, back there at the volcanoes. I thought as much!

BOOK REVIEW: I certainly didn't think that.

WOLF HAAS: Then that's perfect. It's supposed to be the first hint. Just enough so you're not really thinking it yet, but that you somehow –

BOOK REVIEW: – sense it.

WOLF HAAS: (*laughs*)

BOOK REVIEW: We're coming to that. To your sexist terminology.

WOLF HAAS: What do you mean now? Anni's terror-feelings?

BOOK REVIEW: Later. Let's stay with the volcano for a minute. Here you could also draw parallels to Mr. Kowalski's repressed character.

WOLF HAAS: I don't know if I would say he was repressed. Well, I just don't want to over-interpret this so volcanically. I have to admit this was the reason I almost threw out the sentence about the volcanoes, so it wasn't like, ah ha! - repressed guy, and then it all erupts out of him, and so on.

BOOK REVIEW: But you left the sentence in. There it is.

WOLF HAAS: Yes, true. But I packaged it carefully so as not to attract much notice. Anyway, the sentence about the volcano that lifts the cover and pushes the clouds into the stratosphere – well, now that you mention it, it suddenly seems to be a pretty crude representation of Mr. Kowalski's character.

BOOK REVIEW: I never said crude.

WOLF HAAS: In any case – what did I want to say? Anyhow, the sentence about the volcanoes is completely overshadowed by the decisive sentence that follows it directly.

BOOK REVIEW: "You absolutely have to appear as a contestant on *Place Your Bets!"*

WOLF HAAS: You have to imagine that at the moment when every other woman told him, stony-faced, "all you can do is talk about the weather," Claudia the secretary, thoroughly fascinated, says "you absolutely have to go on *Place Your Bets!"*

BOOK REVIEW: And that's how it happened. How much time went by between Claudia's plan, signing her boss up for *Place Your Bet* –

WOLF HAAS: That was more Riemer's plan.

BOOK REVIEW: – and his actual appearance?

WOLF HAAS: Just about half a year.

BOOK REVIEW: You depicted his appearance on Gottschalk's show in minute detail, but other parts of the show, before and after his appearance, you changed radically. I couldn't quite understand what rules you were going by there.

WOLF HAAS: I don't think I changed all that much. I just added the appearance by Phil Collins. In reality, Phil Collins did appear one episode earlier on *Place Your Bets*, and at first I was angry that he had slipped through my fingers. I'm not really sure why I just had to have him in there.

BOOK REVIEW: I read it as a nice contrast to Mr. Kowalski's shy passion, Phil Collins warbling all those phony feelings.

WOLF HAAS: Yes, I think so too.

BOOK REVIEW: Were you ever afraid that Gottschalk could have something against turning up in your novel? Or did you protect yourself somehow by getting the rights? Does the publisher do that for an author?

WOLF HAAS: In my dialect there's this great saying that I rely on in emergencies. "If you don't ask, they can't tell you no."

BOOK REVIEW: I must remember that.

WOLF HAAS: But in all seriousness, why should he stop me? I didn't make anything up. That part of the book is almost journalistic. I got the video from Riemer, who had recorded it. I think I must have watched it about a hundred times. In that part of the book you can find a very faithful description of what I saw on television. How Mr. Kowalski came onstage and began to sweat because he was dressed too warmly. How Gottschalk introduced him to the audience, explained his challenge, made some little joke about "weather-betting" and then quickly began the questions.

BOOK REVIEW: He was probably running out of time.

WOLF HAAS: Yes, presumably. The eternal problem. Maybe also because there's not that much to him. Mr. Kowalski wasn't a raucous contestant. He was actually a bit of a bore.

BOOK REVIEW: You really don't have too much respect for the characters in your novel.

WOLF HAAS: I'm just talking about his television presence. If I really thought he was a bore I wouldn't have written a book about him. Or maybe it was more about the topic. "The Last Bore," maybe that would have been a good title. In any case, to make a long story short, to use Kowalski's favorite expressions –

BOOK REVIEW: That doesn't come up in the book.

WOLF HAAS: Just once, I believe. Where he describes that between the summers, Anni, in those eleven months of his absence, so to speak, had changed from a girl into a woman. In other words, physically –

BOOK REVIEW: Oh yes, right .The breast passage. That was also a bit –

WOLF HAAS: In any case, to make a long story short. Now the short story is getting long again.

BOOK REVIEW: Because I interrupted you.

WOLF HAAS: Doesn't matter.

BOOK REVIEW: Making a long story short?

WOLF HAAS: Gottschalk started right in with his questions.

BOOK REVIEW: You have five questions in your book.

WOLF HAAS: Just as there were in reality. He had to know the weather for five days out of the last fifteen years in Farmach. And he rattled off the first four answers without hesitation. The audience went wild.

BOOK REVIEW: You write that he was ticked off at Gottschalk for interrupting his answers so abruptly.

WOLF HAAS: That was not obvious to the unbiased TV watcher, but once you are aware of it, you see clearly in the video that he's getting annoyed. In the first question Gottschalk interrupted him for the day's high and low temperatures, and the audience loved it. Mr. Kowalski though, in his mind, was barely getting started. He was ready to defend himself on the next questions. When I watched the tape again I thought it was really very clever. The way he began with some unimportant details. Well, the second question was a day in October, I believe.

BOOK REVIEW: The twelfth. You write, "So he couldn't interrupt me too early, this time I began with the less controversial data."

WOLF HAAS: So then he began with cloud formations, cloud density and the direction of air currents, humidity and wind speed, hoarfrost at one thousand three hundred meters, until Gottschalk more or less forced him to fork over the temperature and minutes of daylight by saying, "the man's embarrassing me. None of this is in my notes."

BOOK REVIEW: You say it was almost a journalistic account of what can be seen on the video, but in the first person narrative a lot of the inner world comes out with it. You experience at least as much of his feelings in the situation, on the stage in Westphalia Hall in your book as you do the real action or the external dialogue. Is that purely a poetic fantasy, or was it influenced by your conversations with Mr. Kowalski?

WOLF HAAS: It goes back to the conversations, but naturally I incorporated things that he had said to me in other contexts that fit better here.

BOOK REVIEW: What, for example?

WOLF HAAS: I don't know. Little things. Even in the passage you mentioned where he holds Gottschalk at bay and only names the temperature and minutes of sunlight after he's forced to, I let him casually comment in the book, "temperature and minutes of sunlight, those two false idols of the average weather consumer."

BOOK REVIEW: And that's you, not him. There I've got to say, I thought so. "False idols of the average weather consumer" is somehow a little too well formulated.

WOLF HAAS: It actually came from him. Well, I wouldn't bet my life on it, but I believe "the two false idols of the average weather consumer" is either his or maybe Riemer's. In any case, it's not mine.Mr. Kowalski just said it in a different context, not in the context of Gottschalk's question, and he also didn't say it about temperature and sunlight minutes, but about temperature and precipitation.

BOOK REVIEW: That's much more logical. Temperature and precipitation are definitely the false idols of us average weather consumers. "Sunlight minutes" seems too theoretical.

WOLF HAAS: Exactly. In this passage it is a little illogical, but it didn't fit anywhere else, and I didn't want to deny myself this great expression. In hindsight, I think I could have left it out altogether. When it comes to wording, authors often have their own false idols.

BOOK REVIEW: Oh, I thought that was good. He answered questions three and four just as confidently. And then it happens. I have to say, this was the most problematic passage in the book.

WOLF HAAS: I'm not surprised.

BOOK REVIEW: On the fifth and last question you have Mr. Kowalski say, "I will never forget how Gottschalk smiled when he named the very first day of the fifteen years. As though he had sensed something." Mr. Haas, I ordered the video of the show before our conversation. The first four days Gottschalk asks about are authentic. But the fifth –

WOLF HAAS: – was different. I know. But it was about the effect on him, and it was just the same as if Gottschalk had asked about the very first day of the fifteen years, because on the day that Gottschalk asked about there really was weather similar to the day when the children saw each other for the last time.

BOOK REVIEW: The day everything ended.

WOLF HAAS: Yes, or the day everything began, depending on how you look at it. "Similar weather" would have made the narrative too complex. It wasn't worth it. When you're writing, sometimes you have to make decisions. Here, I wanted it to move quickly. You don't gain anything when I write some intricate bit about the way that the weather Gottschalk asked about reminded him of the day when he went up to the smuggler's den with Anni. It's simply a question of textual economy. Better to tolerate a bit of coincidence than have to read three pages of "reminded him of…"

BOOK REVIEW: And in a pinch you can justify coincidence with the Aunt Emma's saying. Or was it Berta?

WOLF HAAS: Right, Aunt Sefa, exactly. "Otherwise, it wouldn't be a movie."

BOOK REVIEW: So, Gottschalk called out the date and Mr. Kowalski didn't react at all.

WOLF HAAS: No, he did react, but it was only a physical reaction. He started to sweat unbelievably.

BOOK REVIEW: I thought that was really great, the way the question makes him relive the whole Anni catastrophe, and in a second, he's sopping wet. Just like back then! But this time, not because of the rain, but because of Anni's sweater that he was wearing under his sport jacket.

WOLF HAAS: Though I've got to say, you don't know that yet at this point – that this is the sweater that Anni knitted for him.

BOOK REVIEW: You don't find that out until the very end, when the sweater actually saves his life.

WOLF HAAS: Yes. On the live TV appearance it's just that it was too hot for him under the spotlights because he's got a thin sweater on under his jacket. Not that it's Anni's sweater.

BOOK REVIEW: Because, as you write, without a sweater, he "didn't feel properly dressed."

WOLF HAAS: (*laughs*) Yes, he gets that from me. But of course the sweater is a diversionary tactic. He's sweating because of the sweater, okay. And because of the spotlights, but the fact that from one moment to the next, he's soaked is due to –

BOOK REVIEW: – the weather.

WOLF HAAS: Simply to his drawing a blank because Gottschalk's question caught him completely off guard.

BOOK REVIEW: When you read it, you get the impression that he wouldn't have gotten the question at all if not for Gottschalk's help.

WOLF HAAS: That's clear from the video. The way

Gottschalk tries to get him past this mental block. Gottschalk repeats the date and emphasizes over and over, “laaaaate summer,” but Mr. Kowalski just stands there, sweating.

BOOK REVIEW: In his thoughts, he’s far away in his own late summer day fifteen years ago.

WOLF HAAS: In “his” late summer day, I like that.

BOOK REVIEW: When he went up to the smuggler’s den with Anni.

WOLF HAAS: He really drifted off to that unlucky day when he was with Anni for the last time.

BOOK REVIEW: You just see that Gottschalk touches him quickly on the elbow, as if he’s trying to wake him up.

WOLF HAAS: Yes, I think that was the decisive moment. This little nudge brings him back to his senses and he mumbles “weather.” Very softly, but because, out of embarrassment, and in total discomfort, he holds the microphone so close to his face, in order to sort of hide himself behind it, everybody hears very loudly, “Weather!” You could hear it in very last row of the auditorium, and you could hear it all over Germany and Switzerland, all the way to the farthest reaches of Austria, when he said, “weather.”

BOOK REVIEW: That’s all he said.

WOLF HAAS: And Gottschalk reacts with his usual wit. “There’s always weather, but what kind of weather, that’s the question.” And Mr. Kowalski repeats

"Weather." Then the penny drops for Gottschalk.

BOOK REVIEW: A storm.

WOLF HAAS: Exactly. I really admire Gottschalk for this quick thinking. My girlfriend always says she can't understand why I watch the show at all, but there's something about moments like these. Gottschalk just turned this embarrassment into a laugh, taking all the blame himself.

BOOK REVIEW: He's a Bavarian.

WOLF HAAS: Exactly. "I'm, a Bavarian," he says, "and I don't understand *weather*." And so on. He knows he's going to hear it from his old friends when he gets home: "Gottschalk, you damn Prussian." Etcetera.

BOOK REVIEW: Other than this word, Kowalski didn't say anything in response to the fifth question at all.

WOLF HAAS: "Weather." Gottschalk let that count as an answer. Mr. Kowalski was the champion of the evening. That was voted at the end of the show, though, and that was when he really got it. But the way Gottschalk cracked that joke about his Bavarian friends who were going to let him have it because he didn't understand right away that "weather" meant a storm, Kowalski didn't register that at all. The memory had been completely erased. When Riemer showed him the video later he was thunderstruck. He saw and heard the part about Gottschalk's Bavarian friends for the first time on the video, as if he hadn't been there at all!

BOOK REVIEW: You write that he wanted to sink into the earth out of shame. It wasn't clear to me if he was ashamed because he didn't know the answer, or –

WOLF HAAS: It was because he felt that he had been exposed. He thought that everybody knew why he was standing there and what had happened on the last day that he saw Anni.

BOOK REVIEW: How the two of them got caught in the "weather" and –

WOLF HAAS: Yes, right. He felt that he had been unmasked.

BOOK REVIEW: Although Gottschalk didn't know anything about the actual tragedy.

WOLF HAAS: No, of course not. That was just a thing between Anni and Kowalski.

BOOK REVIEW: It seems to me, or, let me put it this way, I have this theory that shame is the shameful secret of the whole story.

WOLF HAAS: I wouldn't go that far, but it is the dominant feeling at this moment. He wanted to sink into the earth out of shame.

BOOK REVIEW: The chapter ends with that wish - to sink into the earth – but I did find it surprising that in this situation of extreme stress, when he draws a blank in front of millions of television viewers, he thinks, of all things, about the citizens' action group that he had worked with over the past few years.

WOLF HAAS: What's more, it was Riemer's to keep the people from the Groundless Citizens' Initiative in check.

BOOK REVIEW: The chapter ends with the lines, "In that moment, I wished more than anything that our friends from the Groundless" Citizens' Initiative had been right."

WOLF HAAS: "Friends." That's a good one.

BOOK REVIEW: And then it goes on: "How nice it would have been if a poorly closed mine shaft had opened beneath the auditorium and graciously swallowed me up."

WOLF HAAS: Yes, the shame of it all. He really wasn't doing too well at this moment. He didn't even register how the audience was cheering for him.

BOOK REVIEW: But it was your clear intention to let him sink into the floor at the end of this chapter. Or, to put it another way, it wasn't an accident that you put the image of him sinking into the floor at the end of the chapter.

WOLF HAAS: Well, there's a little bit of foreshadowing in all this.

BOOK REVIEW: Of his impending downfall.

WOLF HAAS: Maybe not directly to his downfall. I just liked that here he, metaphorically, sinks into the earth and at the end of the book, the earth spits him back, you know?

BOOK REVIEW: Yes, and while we're on the topic, I have to say there's a huge difference between this and the eruptions at the end of the novel. He doesn't really sink here. The way you're saying it, it almost sounds as if the earth under the auditorium really does swallow him up.

WOLF HAAS: No, of course not. He just wishes it would. And there's that old superstition about things like this: be careful what you wish for.

Day Three

BOOK REVIEW: Mr. Haas, with the "weather" that Gottschalk inadvertently referred to, we've reached the core of the whole story.

WOLF HAAS: I don't think a story necessarily has a core.

BOOK REVIEW: But it's hard to disagree with the fact that the whole story twines around this one day when Anni and Vittorio get caught in the storm.

WOLF HAAS: Cores, twining – now we're getting into botany.

BOOK REVIEW: That fits well with the excursion the two fifteen-year-olds make into the world of botany that day.

WOLF HAAS: Yes. Ha ha. You are now entering a pun-free zone.

BOOK REVIEW: I didn't notice that, but I did notice when I was reading that in this decisive passage you shift your scene to a secondary location. The high tension wires the two young hikers pass under before they get caught in the storm.

WOLF HAAS: It was a stroke of luck for me as an author that the path the two took that day –

BOOK REVIEW: – up to the smuggler's den –

WOLF HAAS: – yes, that the path up to the smuggler's den, passes under the high tension wires. It's not far to the smuggler's den from there.

BOOK REVIEW: A stroke of luck because you could mirror the discharge of the lightning with artificial electricity. You don't like nature all that much.

WOLF HAAS: Nature doesn't really like me either.

BOOK REVIEW: I'm just trying to understand why the high tension wires are so important for you.

WOLF HAAS: I don't know. Have you ever seen high tension wires in the mountains?

BOOK REVIEW: I think I can imagine pretty well after reading your book.

WOLF HAAS: They are really something. In Austria, we say otherworldly. From another place, uncanny.

BOOK REVIEW: In other words, from the beyond.

WOLF HAAS: Yes. Eerie, somehow.

BOOK REVIEW: When both children lose their innocence, they go under the high tension wires for the first time.

WOLF HAAS: Lose their innocence, that's good. But I must raise a quick objection. The novel doesn't tell the story of a couple of lovers who walk up a mountain and happen to, wink wink, nudge nudge, go under the high tension wires that they'd always been afraid of.

BOOK REVIEW: No?

WOLF HAAS: No! The passage about the high tension wires is, above all, about the insects! A storm always announces itself through the bloodlust of insects. Both of the kids walk up to the first bench as they'd done almost every day in this final summer, in all innocence, so to speak.

BOOK REVIEW: In the direction of the smuggler's den.

WOLF HAAS: Right, in the direction of the smuggler's den, but only the first couple of hundred meters. The first bench is a good distance before the high tension wires. Even the third bench comes before the wires. The first is a lot closer to the village than to the smuggler's den. They both go up to the first bench almost every day, particularly in their last summer, but they practically never go any farther. Very rarely do they go to the second bench. Never to the third, which is practically next to the high tension wires.

BOOK REVIEW: Even at the first bench, nobody can see them.

WOLF HAAS: It's not really far to the first bench, and it's also not too steep yet. It's a fifteen minute walk, but this time the sweat's streaming off them at the first bench because it's so unbelievably muggy. And the insects are really going at both of them.

BOOK REVIEW: By the way, I thought this passage was a little racy, the way you call attention to Anni's delicate skin.

WOLF HAAS: I didn't write "delicate skin." It's "thin skin."

BOOK REVIEW: Yes, right. "Her skin was so thin that insect stingers could penetrate it effortlessly and her blood -"

WOLF HAAS: It was once suggested to me that Anni almost never appears in the book, that she never sufficiently expresses herself and so on, that she's just a projected image, but that goes too far.

BOOK REVIEW: I don't know if that's really an argument. Here's a young woman who is otherwise barely characterized, and of all things you take her delicate skin –

WOLF HAAS: Thin skin.

BOOK REVIEW: In the case of the "effortlessly" penetrating stingers, one is tempted to say –

WOLF HAAS: Funnily enough, that's something Anni told me herself. Literally! That the insects always attack her because she has thin skin. She really does have thin skin, skin you can see the veins through, really insect-friendly, I've got to say.

BOOK REVIEW: But you call attention to it at every opportunity. That's no excuse, even if that is the way that things really were.

WOLF HAAS: That's true. I have to give myself credit for once. In this case I tried, paradoxically, to camouflage the statement because I took Anni's explanation literally.

BOOK REVIEW: Very dialectical.

WOLF HAAS: I could have made it easy for myself and simply said that the pedantic view is just typical of the dry narrative style of an engineer.

BOOK REVIEW: But?

WOLF HAAS: I could say, a typical engineer, then there's another cold mechanical explanation of how the stinger penetrates more easily through thin skin.

BOOK REVIEW: But?

WOLF HAAS: But actually the opposite is true! Precisely because I cite Anni word for word, the reader is alienated. Alienation through realism! Because in reality, insects go for the smell.

BOOK REVIEW: Now you're just saying that the reference to thin skin was to disguise the fact that Anni's smell was so interesting.

WOLF HAAS: And they would have been all over me if I had written that her beguiling scent attracted the insects! Then that just goes in the direction of hormone levels or sexual –

BOOK REVIEW: And you wanted to avoid that.

WOLF HAAS: The aroma accompanies the cigarettes, at best. Because Anni conjures up a half-full pack of cigarettes she stole from her father's truck. They light two cigarettes to keep the annoying insects away.

BOOK REVIEW: Also a clear, erotic signal. You write that it was the first cigarette for both of them.

WOLF HAAS: Of course, at that age there's still something secret and forbidden about it. Back then, at least.

BOOK REVIEW: "Back then."

WOLF HAAS: For me it's not about the erotic subtext though. It's very concretely about the fact that the smoke didn't keep the insects away. The insects are so wild that the smoke didn't faze them at all. They absolutely cling to their skin.

BOOK REVIEW: To Anni's skin.

WOLF HAAS: Normally they didn't go after him as much, but on this day they went for his skin too.

BOOK REVIEW: The insects are so wild that they almost start crying. Are they really that aggressive in the mountains? Somehow I can't imagine that.

WOLF HAAS: They're brutal before a storm. The gadfly stingers really burn so much that you scream. The horseflies can even sting you through your jeans. And of course the insects' aggressiveness naturally carried over to them.

BOOK REVIEW: I find it very characteristic of you as an author that the fight is ignited by a linguistic discussion.

WOLF HAAS: Yes, well. I factored that out of the book entirely. Naturally there was constant verbal friction between the German summer boy and the local girl. That would have gotten out of control. It doesn't interest me anymore, but in this situation she made fun of him again because of his funny name for the gadflies.

BOOK REVIEW: Blind cuckoos.

WOLF HAAS: Yes, he calls the common horsefly a blind cuckoo. I really liked the name and I definitely wanted to include it.

BOOK REVIEW: Fate encounters them in the form of a blind cuckoo.

WOLF HAAS: An author just can't leave something like that out.

BOOK REVIEW: The blind cuckoo is not just the sole witness to their momentous excursion, it also drives the plot forward.

WOLF HAAS: Because they start to slap the bloodsuckers off each other. It isn't long before they start slapping each other's bare skin.

BOOK REVIEW: Then the game turns bloody serious.

WOLF HAAS: Naturally it's a dangerous game. On the one hand, it's a loving gesture, brushing away a fly before someone gets stung. On the other hand, it depends on how hard you hit. Kids like to take that as a pretense to really slap someone hard on the back or bare thigh or, best of all, right in the face. Wherever they can, even when there's no fly. No blind cuckoo, just a blind slap, so to speak.

BOOK REVIEW: But Vittorio and Anni weren't exactly kids anymore.

WOLF HAAS: No. Well, in transition, I'd say. They'd been smacking the insects off from each other for a while, and –

BOOK REVIEW: You describe it almost like a ritual dance.

WOLF HAAS: When blood was running down Anni's cheek, though, she didn't think it was so funny anymore.

BOOK REVIEW: But it was just the horsefly's blood.

WOLF HAAS: Sure. But strictly speaking it was also Anni's blood because the critter had sucked it out of her.

BOOK REVIEW: A philosophical question.

WOLF HAAS: She was just being theatrical, pretending she was really mad because there was blood running down her cheek. First the quarrel about the insect names, ha ha blind cuckoo ha ha horsefly, and so on, and now there's blood flowing. And then there was the bloated fly that Vittorio had crushed on her cheek.

BOOK REVIEW: Speaking of bloated, a friend of mine once told me about this awful Austrian expression. How does it go? As full as a toilet cigarette?

WOLF HAAS: Yeah, as full as a crapper cig. But it means drunk. Well, you know, "crapper" is the toilet, and because –

BOOK REVIEW: I know, I can remember the awful description.

WOLF HAAS: – well, the men in the bathroom – I'm a

non-smoker, myself – but they throw the butts in the urinal and of course they swell up. It's a particularly extreme kind of bloating.

BOOK REVIEW: Thanks for clarifying that for me again. As a woman I don't understand the whole urinal thing. But, anyway, Anni is being theatrical while the insect blood runs down her check. That doesn't send her off down the mountain, but instead, up they go.

WOLF HAAS: That was precisely the thing with the high tension wires. That's why I said the high tension wires come into the story because of the insects. The high tension wires were the subject of a long-standing fight between them.

BOOK REVIEW: Every time they went for a walk, they would reach a point where they would argue about whether or not they could hear the high tension wires yet.

WOLF HAAS: It wasn't really possible to test it objectively.

BOOK REVIEW: Here's the thing, though. One day Anni begins to think that she is "feeling" the high tension wires well before they could be heard.

WOLF HAAS: (*laughs*)

BOOK REVIEW: You're using Anni's "feeling" the high tension wires as another one of your jabs at the female.

WOLF HAAS: Maybe jab is going too far, the bit about "feeling," that's, of course, a topic or a theme I can't avoid when it's handed to me.

BOOK REVIEW: Although "terror feeling" is blunt expression, as you use it there.

WOLF HAAS: I got too deeply involved in the text. Well, I guarantee that the expression "terror feeling" didn't come from Mr. Kowalski. He was really amazed that Anni could already "feel" the high tension wires before he could even hear them at all.

BOOK REVIEW: In the book it says that the high tension wires could be heard for the first time at midway on the trail between the first and second benches, and, on some days, only after the second bench. Now and then you could even hear them a few meters after the first bench. Is there really such a difference?

WOLF HAAS: I think so. Depends on which direction the current is flowing.

BOOK REVIEW: That's a joke, right?

WOLF HAAS: You're a real lightning rod.

BOOK REVIEW: What?

WOLF HAAS: Sorry. That was stupid. Forget it.

BOOK REVIEW: But I want to know.

WOLF HAAS: An Austrian soccer player said that once to a German TV reporter in a famous interview: "You're a lightning rod." He meant quick on the uptake.

BOOK REVIEW: Aha. Thanks for the flowers.

WOLF HAAS: The German reporter actually asked him why it was taking so long to extend the contract with his German club and the soccer player said, in a very Viennese singsong, "We have to negotiate because the club wants to pay me more than I'm worth." And to that the reporter said, "You're kidding me, right?" And then the player answered, "you're a lightning rod."

BOOK REVIEW: Nice.

WOLF HAAS: For us, that's as well-known as "I be done now."

BOOK REVIEW: Who was the player? Hans Kranker?

WOLF HAAS: No, let's quit this nonsense. Where were we?

BOOK REVIEW: Why sometime you could hear the high tension wires at the first bench, but at other times, not even at the second.

WOLF HAAS: Never directly at the first bench. There they were safe, but sometimes right after the first curve, when you went in the direction of the high tension wires, in other words, toward the smuggler's den.

BOOK REVIEW: My lightning wit leads me to conclude that it really depends on the direction the wind is blowing.

WOLF HAAS: I would say so. And the two of them made a game out of it for years: who could hear the high tension wires first. I liked the game so much because you can't prove it anyway. But once, when he didn't want to believe at first that she could hear something, the girl made up this cock-and-bull story.

BOOK REVIEW: She could “feel” it.

WOLF HAAS: Exactly. In the palms of her hands.

BOOK REVIEW: Prickling.

WOLF HAAS: He couldn’t compete with that. He didn’t feel anything. No prickling. And he was just too honest to say he could feel it too.

BOOK REVIEW: Too much of an egghead. Telltale signs of an engineer-to-be.

WOLF HAAS: He was also too good-hearted to suspect her of pretending. Instead, he was convinced that girls just feel it. They’re more sensitive, etc.

BOOK REVIEW: This generous view isn’t just the author talking. You write that women just seem to feel anything that suits them.

WOLF HAAS: No, I certainly don’t write anything like that! Now you’re goading me because I said that thing about the lightning rod.

BOOK REVIEW: That sentence is word for word from your book.

WOLF HAAS: Yes, but it’s a sentence from Riemer in an entirely different context. In this passage, it’s only about their game – to see who could hear the high tension wires first. Anni always turned around as soon as she heard the buzzing.

BOOK REVIEW: The buzzing was the signal.

WOLF HAAS: For departure. Because it hurt her ears.

BOOK REVIEW: And the expression “terror feeling”? Is that colloquial Riemer or colloquial Wolf Haas?

WOLF HAAS: I already admitted it. “Terror feeling” should have been left out of the book. As far as I’m concerned, it’s mine. I sometimes think it’s bizarre when people say things like, “I sense it; you’ll feel it too.” People only are going to feel what they feel.

BOOK REVIEW: That upsets you.

WOLF HAAS: I just don’t like it when people spontaneously start feeling all over the place. As far as the book goes, though, there’s another reason why I emphasize it. It’s because on this day things are suddenly turned around. All of a sudden, he’s the one who hears the wires first.

BOOK REVIEW: Or thinks he hears.

WOLF HAAS: At the first bench! Where they could never be heard before!

BOOK REVIEW: And now it’s Anni who says, “Bull. You can’t hear anything.”

WOLF HAAS: And suddenly Vittorio claims he even feels them. Behind the buzzing of the insects there is another buzzing in the air. He feels it prickling in his palms and Anni says there’s nothing to feel – it doesn’t make your palms prickle.

BOOK REVIEW: On this day, when there is erotic tension in the air for the first time, suddenly it's Vittorio who claims to feel the high tension wires. I took that to mean that he wanted to turn back. He was actually afraid of the situation and was trying to signal Anni to turn around.

WOLF HAAS: But Anni didn't play along. Maybe she was still upset about the blood on her cheek. In any case, she said that she heard and felt nothing. And she looked pensively up at the blue sky as if she were listening.

BOOK REVIEW: It was still a blue sky?

WOLF HAAS: Not a cloud in the heavens! It was just noon. That was what was so crazy about the oppressive heat and the insect attack. In the Alps that usually happens in the afternoons at the earliest.

BOOK REVIEW: So, we're trying to create a kind of "high noon" mood?

WOLF HAAS: It was just exactly noon. There's a simple reason why I know that. Mr. Kowalski told me that they could hear the noon bells from the village church unusually loud as far up as the first bench. That's an important detail because –

BOOK REVIEW: – because then it's improbable that the wind was coming from the direction of the high tension wires.

WOLF HAAS: Precisely. Either that, or the wind shifted direction extremely fast. In any case, it was just twelve o'clock, late summer, blue sky, no shade. And when the noon bells faded away, the buzzing of the insects was in the air again, louder than before, and behind that, there was the buzzing of the high tension wires.

BOOK REVIEW: And Anni continues to deny it.

WOLF HAAS: The same old bickering. Vittorio says again that he hears the high tension wires and Anni repeats, not at the first bench! And Vittorio repeats that he feels them, and Anni says you can't hear anything and you can't feel anything. And she looks up at the blue sky and says -

BOOK REVIEW: – with this penetrating glance that earlier on in the book was always so important –

WOLF HAAS: With that stupid local look. The one the villagers use when they make their weather forecasts for the tourists.

BOOK REVIEW: As we know from Anni's father, the head of the mountain rescue team, who shoots that look to Mr. Kowalski senior when he asks if the weather will hold for his hike the next day.

WOLF HAAS: Yes, exactly. And now his fifteen-year-old daughter is gazing up at the blue sky with this same look and saying with the seriousness of experience, "There's weather coming."

BOOK REVIEW: In this passage, you really believe she's just saying it to show off. To be a village girl and make Vittorio feel the weakness of his position.

WOLF HAAS: I'm glad it comes across that way. At this point, you side more with Vittorio because the whole situation is getting to be too much for him. He's not only just a stranger, the "summer kid," but he's also her age and so, as far as development goes at that age, the more immature of the two, so he's doubly handicapped. Then she let him have it because of the bloody smack on her cheek. And now Anni's gazing up at the blue sky with this villager's look, saying, as if to mock him, "There's weather coming."

BOOK REVIEW: Actually, that would have been a reason for them to go back to the village. You emphasize the danger of the weather in the Alps for mountain climbers many times in the book. By the way, you don't necessarily have to beat that point to death. We get it, even though we're flatland Krauts.

WOLF HAAS: With the two of them it's not about mountain climbers in that sense. They're only about fifteen minutes away from the village. But nonetheless, when you're out in nature, a storm is never fun. Even though you're only fifteen minutes away, suddenly you're cut off from civilization.

BOOK REVIEW: But the two don't turn around and go back. Instead, they go farther in the direction of the high tension wires despite the buzzing and despite Anni's weather forecast.

WOLF HAAS: Yes. They go up to the second bench. First bench, second bench, third bench. Those are the stations before the high tension wires.

BOOK REVIEW: Vittorio always counts them like that. I wonder whether he got this counting compulsion from you, or you got it from him.

WOLF HAAS: In this case it's only important because they've usually only gotten as far as the first bench. That was sort of their living room. Just the right distance from the adult world. Not really visible from the village, but not too far away. And only rarely did they climb the steep path up to the second bench. That was inside the area where they could feel the buzzing.

BOOK REVIEW: And this time they don't just go to the second, they go all the way up to the third bench.

WOLF HAAS: Right, for the first time! They had never been to the third bench before. That's fifty meters beyond the high tension wires. Really uncomfortable. I don't get why someone put a bench up there.

BOOK REVIEW: Even though there was this horrible buzzing.

WOLF HAAS: First and foremost, the buzzing was just a pretense for their laziness. For me, it was about the particular sluggishness of fifteen-year-olds. You're never as lazy as when you're that age. It's such a massive torpor that I get tired just thinking about it.

BOOK REVIEW: Well, at that age I was training for the 400 meter.

WOLF HAAS: You missed out! Normally a person is lethargic at that age. It's an excessive loginess. You lie all day in front of the TV or whatever, go to the pool, or today they hang out in front of the computer. They just don't move.

BOOK REVIEW: Now I understand why you emphasize that they go up to the third bench, and even up to the high tension wires.

WOLF HAAS: I couldn't turn laziness into a major theme, my readers would fall asleep!

BOOK REVIEW: I always wondered why it meant so much that they go farther, even though the walk couldn't have lasted more than half an hour.

WOLF HAAS: No, not more than that. Roughly ten minutes from the first to the second bench. And a good quarter of an hour from the second to the third bench, which is directly up there at the high tension wires. But the path is very steep, and when you're lazy it's an ordeal. Especially when it's so muggy. It's like a steep climb inside a greenhouse.

BOOK REVIEW: That's why they're both soaked to the skin before it even starts to rain.

WOLF HAAS: Before there's even a cloud in the sky! It was still blue sky and Vittorio almost ran up the mountain. He was absolutely determined to go in the direction of the high tension wires until Anni admitted it.

BOOK REVIEW: That behind the buzzing of the insects there was a palpable buzzing from the high tension wires.

WOLF HAAS: But not from weather, which she talked about to show off her intuition. He'd simply had enough. To him this felt like the tortoise and the hare. Once he found that he was ahead in the hearing competition, she raised the stakes to feeling. And now, when he's playing along and keeping up with this sensing of the wires, suddenly she's onto something else.

BOOK REVIEW: Weather sensitivity.

WOLF HAAS: There's weather coming! Actually, that was the first time he stood up for himself and didn't swallow everything she said.

BOOK REVIEW: I can only agree partially. When you're reading you also get the feeling she's provoking him. If she hadn't denied so vehemently that it was the high tension wires that caused the prickling in the hands, they could have turned back in good faith.

WOLF HAAS: But Anni didn't admit it.

BOOK REVIEW: Right. That's my point. In that situation, if someone wants to turn around they just say, okay, you win, so let's turn around now.

WOLF HAAS: Yes, I think you're right. He just wanted her to admit it was the high tension wires. But maybe that's what she wanted from him. At any rate, they kept going farther and farther up. Because he wanted to prove it to her. Because once they could hear the wires undeniably loud, she didn't leave off: it's not the wires, there's weather coming. There wasn't a cloud in the sky

BOOK REVIEW: Terror feeling.

WOLF HAAS: Well, the weather proved her correct sooner than she would have liked.

BOOK REVIEW: It gets dark even before they get to the high tension wires.

WOLF HAAS: At the third bench it was already

overcast. In the middle of a sunny summer day, the light fades in five minutes.

BOOK REVIEW: In the book it says three minutes.

WOLF HAAS: I could have written one minute. That's how you experience it. When you're standing on a mountainside half an hour from civilization, closer to the tree line than the village, it always happens fast. *Out of the blue into the dark,* as Neil Young sings.

BOOK REVIEW: *Out of the blue into the dark*. Nice. What song's that from?

WOLF HAAS: Unfortunately I couldn't quote the line because Stephen King used it. Maybe that's why it came to mind. Because it's a bit Stephen King-ish when you're standing on a mountain like that, and in the middle of the day it just gets dark. I have to say that the high tension wires themselves radiate a certain feeling of horror.

BOOK REVIEW: "Otherworldly."

WOLF HAAS: Walking under buzzing high tension wires even on a clear day is something you want to get over with as quickly as possible. Especially when, in the middle of a bright sunny day, it gets dark in the course of a minute.

BOOK REVIEW: Mr. Haas, I take it that you know the famous dissertation by F. C. Delius?

WOLF HAAS: *The Hero and his Weather.* What makes you think I'm familiar with it? It's not really all that well-known.

BOOK REVIEW: It's obvious I'm not completely wrong. I would be amazed if, after working on the topic for a year, you hadn't come across it.

WOLF HAAS: I was tempted to borrow an epigraph from *The Hero and his Weather,* but epigraphs like that don't send good signals.

BOOK REVIEW: Your book does have an epigraph.

WOLF HAAS: But a wedding song is different from philosophical stuff that you skim and only partially understand.

BOOK REVIEW: The wedding song also provides some sneaky foreshadowing of Anni's wedding. You're hoping the whole time that it refers to a different wedding!

WOLF HAAS: I think it's a pretty song. And this popular wedding song begins with a line about the weather – I couldn't miss the chance to include it. And I didn't just want it in the book, I wanted it on the first page.

BOOK REVIEW: "Through rain, or wind"

WOLF HAAS: "– or rimy weather." Is that understandable?

BOOK REVIEW: Yes, icy weather.

WOLF HAAS: "Through rain, or wind, or rimy weather"

BOOK REVIEW: “we’ll be fine if we’re together.”

WOLF HAAS: It’s nuts, but I’ve got goose bumps. Of course it’s a little kitschy, but –

BOOK REVIEW: – as a quotation, it works for you.

WOLF HAAS: Yes, I suppose.

BOOK REVIEW: The reason I asked about *The Hero and his Weather* was that your dissertation is always mentioned in reviews. On the *Philosophy of Language and the Basis of Concrete Poetry*.

WOLF HAAS: But in my case it was more about the justification of grammatical errors. The academic license to make mistakes.

BOOK REVIEW: Mr. Haas, even though you’re making fun of it, I don’t understand how, with this background, you manage to describe the weather for twenty pages on end.

WOLF HAAS: It can’t be twenty pages.

BOOK REVIEW: It is. I counted. It starts with the sudden darkening of the sky. You describe how the sun disappears while the two of them are approaching the high tension wires.

WOLF HAAS: Evaporates.

BOOK REVIEW: Yes, I thought it was very beautiful that you write that the sun evaporates. Then you tell how the high tension wires buzz louder and louder as it gets darker at midday. You describe how, with every step, the electric cables get louder but harder to see. That lasts for pages! You write about the way the earth reflects back the heat of the completely evaporated sun. You write how it gets more and more muggy and oppressive. You write the way the cloud cover stands over them like a bell jar. And then you describe the counting, for seven pages.

WOLF HAAS: I see you counted too.

BOOK REVIEW: Yes, the pages.

WOLF HAAS: Now, I would argue the exact opposite. Namely, that I didn't describe the storm itself at all, because it's impossible. The threat, which, in the truest sense of the word, hangs in the air, the fear of death that you feel as a hiker, that isn't even touched on. It's always played down. That's sort of why I devoted so much space to the high tension wires, the artificial storm, you know, the instant coffee. And the counting is just some kind of ritualized way to deal with, you know, the insanity of the alpine storm –

BOOK REVIEW: Yes, that's all well and good, but it's a question of –

WOLF HAAS: Of going over the top.

BOOK REVIEW: Somehow, yes.

WOLF HAAS: I'm particularly fascinated by the counting down to the storm as an attempt to rationalize their fear. To keep the storm at bay by counting the seconds. You can grasp the threat if you can at least figure out how fast it's approaching.

BOOK REVIEW: Of course that's an illusion though. You can never get hold of it.

WOLF HAAS: You can if you count with your fingers.

BOOK REVIEW: We are in the pun-free zone.

WOLF HAAS: I just mean the need for control.

BOOK REVIEW: The need for control clearly expresses itself through the counting, but the way you explain it is highly mathematical, why three seconds pass between lightning and thunder. The storm is exactly one thousand forty meters away.

WOLF HAAS: Yes. One thousand twenty.

BOOK REVIEW: One thousand twenty. You see, I would have gone too close to the lightning.

WOLF HAAS: Well, it isn't highly "mathematical." I'm not a great mathematician, but it occurs to me that as soon as there's something with counting, people immediately say it's highly mathematical. Clearly there's no such thing as normal math. Forget about simple arithmetic. I just write how you can figure out the distance to a storm by counting seconds. That doesn't have anything to do with mathematics.

BOOK REVIEW: It isn't higher math, you're right. In the middle of a love story, though, the constant calculating is a little off-putting.

WOLF HAAS: For me it was about the fear that causes people to start calculating the distance of the lightning. The calculations are so easy because the boom is delayed

340 meters per second. That's sound. For light, by the way, it's three hundred million meters. I didn't include that at all. The light just gets there instantly, so to speak.

BOOK REVIEW: You simplified it for us average weather consumers.

WOLF HAAS: And the boom sneaks up behind it at 340 meters per second, so for example when it takes six seconds, then the lightning is still 2040 meters away.

BOOK REVIEW: There you go again.

WOLF HAAS: You don't like this passage.

BOOK REVIEW: When I was reading I just wanted to get through it faster. One gets scared for the children! You describe the approach of the storm for pages. The way Anni and Vittorio keep counting the seconds between the lightning and the thunder, which is still far away at the beginning: twenty-one, twenty-two, twenty-three.

WOLF HAAS: Twenty-four, twenty-five, twenty-six, twenty-seven, twenty-

BOOK REVIEW: In the beginning it's impressive, and somehow maybe suspenseful, but you write that the storm raced toward them, but by counting down meter by meter, you get the impression when you're reading that it creeps up on them slowly.

WOLF HAAS: To be honest, the editor cut a few pages. Twenty-one, twenty-two, twenty-three, twenty-four, for me those are very tantalizing moments in the text.

BOOK REVIEW: I can tell.

WOLF HAAS: But that's not my preference for –

BOOK REVIEW: – for counting –

WOLF HAAS: Ha ha. For meaningless passages. My God, people drive motorcycles through the desert for weeks and everyone understands. They even pay for it! But a few pages with twenty-one, twenty-two, twenty-three, and you're immediately declared insane.

BOOK REVIEW: You said it's just your preference for meaningless passages. What else?

WOLF HAAS: It builds up a certain tension. They count to nine, well, twenty-nine, and then just to twenty-eight, twenty-seven – the storm's getting closer – then twenty-six.

BOOK REVIEW: And for variety's sake, it's twenty-eight again.

WOLF HAAS: Well, of course, in nature, not everything happens in such a linear way. A storm approaches, recedes, gets closer again. Like cat and mouse. And then, *boom*!

BOOK REVIEW: But you wouldn't have me believe that you are an author who appreciates a photo-realistic description of an alpine storm.

WOLF HAAS: Well, that's the funny thing. Twenty-five – and then *boom*! The pounce.

BOOK REVIEW: Loss of control.

WOLF HAAS: When you count, you think you can control the storm, but it moves closer, and apart from these little fluctuations, which are probably just the result of imprecise counting, wishful thinking that it will move away, it just keeps getting closer, from ten to nine to eight to seven to six to five seconds. But then, not to four! Not to three! Not to two!

BOOK REVIEW: Because all at once it's there. Just like that.

WOLF HAAS: Suddenly, it's on your doorstep.

BOOK REVIEW: That means you have described the slow approach in such detail –

WOLF HAAS: Not slow! Gradual. Controlled. At first the storm follows the rules. It approaches with incredible speed, but at a pace that makes sense. From four kilometers to three kilometers takes just as long as from three kilometers to two. It moves incredibly fast, but predictably. And then suddenly it stops following the rules.

BOOK REVIEW: Well, I'll tell you honestly, for me the storm's rapid approach described almost in super slow-motion is a bit over the top. A little too much! It just takes too long!

WOLF HAAS: That's how fast it went in reality, though.

BOOK REVIEW: Right! I'm an impatient person. It didn't really grab me until the downpour started.

WOLF HAAS: Which is an optical illusion. The real downpour is practically absent from the text. I take it you mean the second before.

BOOK REVIEW: Yes, the second before. The long second before it comes down when you're really holding your breath.

WOLF HAAS: That passage was the easiest to write. Have you ever experienced a real alpine storm?

BOOK REVIEW: Well, I've been to the mountains often, in Austria, too. The storms there really scared me, but thank God I never experienced a violent torrent like the one in your book. If I had, I wouldn't be sitting here today. I would have died of fright or gone crazy.

WOLF HAAS: My goal was to have the reader really experience the cardiac arrhythmia that happens when you're in a storm. Or the second before, when the air feels sucked out.

BOOK REVIEW: When I was reading, the moment was really ominous when, for the first time, they look at the high tension tower and see the danger sign banging non-stop against the metal in the wind.

WOLF HAAS: Which is a harmless thing, in and of itself.

BOOK REVIEW: Yes, the thing is harmless when you just take it as a tin-plated sign clanging against the metal high tension tower. But there's also a message on the sign.

WOLF HAAS: DANGER! Even in nice weather it gives

you the chills. You're hiking through an idyllic landscape and suddenly black on yellow DANGER! on some electric tower that looks like it belongs in science fiction. Right there where you'd be more likely to be threatened by a wild animal than by high tension wires. The whole thing has the feeling of an atomic waste dump – you don't even need the storm to feel unwelcome here.

BOOK REVIEW: But the storm was there.

WOLF HAAS: Not yet!

BOOK REVIEW: But the sky had darkened. The two of them can only read the sign when the lightning flashes. And the whole time you're asking yourself why they don't just turn around, why they don't run back down. Why do they keep going toward the high tension wires?

WOLF HAAS: Yes, exactly. Instead, they run up to them. Running, in and of itself, is a mortal sin for climbers. Even when you're in a hurry, you don't run in the mountains. That was mother's milk to Anni.

BOOK REVIEW: Anni took command again once the storm picked up.

WOLF HAAS: I think they ran just because they wanted to put the power lines behind them once and for all. There's also the fear that the tower is going to get hit, and when you're standing right next to it –

BOOK REVIEW: But the storm is still too far away for that. You describe a flash of lightning that quivers across the sky and hits in a field across the valley. At that point you comment that it looks, to a "normal weather consumer," as if the lightning is striking from the sky down to the earth. I looked it up and you're right.

WOLF HAAS: That the air discharges in all directions?

BOOK REVIEW: I didn't believe your claim that the lightning is just as likely to travel up to the sky as down to the ground.

WOLF HAAS: Why else would I say it?

BOOK REVIEW: I'm still wondering if the emphasis on the direction of the lightning somehow held a kind of male-female symbolism for you.

WOLF HAAS: No, for God's sake. That's really how it is. Lightning bolts strike from the sky down as often as from the earth up. They don't weigh anything, so why should they have to go down? They discharge in all directions!

BOOK REVIEW: I know. But it would also make complete sense as foreshadowing. When you think about what happens between Anni and Vittorio –

WOLF HAAS: What fascinated me was just the way our eyes deceive us. The two of them are desperately trying to control the storm by counting – comparing the visual and auditory information they're getting from their senses, and their eyes are fooling them from the start.

BOOK REVIEW: You write that the lightning bolt that shot across the sky for one second was still two kilometers away.

WOLF HAAS: Approximately two kilometers. Vittorio

counted six seconds and Anni five. Still, the counting is imprecise. This was the moment when they ran past the high tension tower.

BOOK REVIEW: In your book it says that the high tension tower lit up like a Las Vegas light show. Have you ever been to Vegas?

WOLF HAAS: No, but Kowalski was there once with Riemer.

BOOK REVIEW: They actually have an Eiffel Tower there. I couldn't help thinking about it when I read this passage.

WOLF HAAS: In reality the pole didn't light up on its own. The metal just reflected the lightning that shot across the sky.

BOOK REVIEW: When you're reading, you keep expecting the danger to come from the high tension wires because of the DANGER sign and everything. I thought the lightning might strike the tower or something like that. Or a high tension wire might snap!

WOLF HAAS: That always gives me the creeps when I'm near power lines, that a fallen electrical cable might accidentally charge the ground under my feet. This is complete idiocy, of course. The DANGER sign only seems so threatening because it was poorly attached at one corner. That's why it bangs so loudly against the metal, but of course nothing happens. It's only dangerous if you climb the tower.

BOOK REVIEW: But neither of them did that. They came out safely on the other side of the high tension wires.

WOLF HAAS: It's just a few meters. Twenty, maybe. They ran under the power lines and up the slope. On the other side, the world looked exactly the same. This is something that had fascinated Vittorio from a very young age: the way the world looked the same on the other side when they used to cross over the Austrian border.

BOOK REVIEW: That fascinated me as a child when I drove with my parents to visit my grandmother in Holland.

WOLF HAAS: Border crossings are always an incredible disappointment.

BOOK REVIEW: In the meantime, the two had other problems. Anni wanted to reach the safety of her father's smuggler's den.

WOLF HAAS: For me it was the hardest thing to judge, what Anni was planning at this moment. Whether she had meant to go to the smuggler's den from the beginning, or just since it had gotten dark. I also tried to leave that open-ended. Maybe that's also a weakness of the novel. In my personal opinion, it was a crazy mix of intention and emotion.

BOOK REVIEW: A combination of fear and lust?

WOLF HAAS: She was afraid of the storm, that much is clear. She knew that they definitely needed to find shelter fast, but she enjoyed scaring Vittorio by constantly pushing him. Maybe she never got over this apparent advantage. She had to continue feeling superior.

BOOK REVIEW: At this point they could have turned and run back to the village.

WOLF HAAS: That would have been certain death for them, though, for sure. Thank God they didn't run down the mountain. On the other side of the high tension wires they stopped to catch their breath and look down into the valley.

BOOK REVIEW: It hadn't rained there yet.

WOLF HAAS: Not a single drop. I was tempted to claim in the novel that on the other side of the wires it suddenly started to rain, as if it were some kind of ominous weathershed.

BOOK REVIEW: No, that would have been too contrived.

WOLF HAAS: Really. And besides, it wasn't like that. They still hadn't felt a single drop. Usually there are those minutes before a storm when it sprinkles for a few seconds, then it stops, then sprinkles again. Indecisive moments before a storm are quite normal, but the storm was still too far away for that. It was still five seconds away, so almost two kilometers.

BOOK REVIEW: You describe those seconds before it came down as an almost mystical moment.

WOLF HAAS: Well okay, but its not automatically a mystical moment every time a light flashes across the sky.

BOOK REVIEW: But you don't describe the lightning as regular bolts, the quick flashes of light across the sky everyone is familiar with. Instead, the entire chain of hills below them is unnaturally illuminated for several seconds, and the very same bolt of lightning seems to hover over several hills without losing its power.

WOLF HAAS: I wouldn't necessarily say mystical. But in view of the other things that happened –

BOOK REVIEW: The mystical element doesn't just come from the flash of lightning that lasts so long. There's also an absence of thunder.

WOLF HAAS: Yes. The two of them start counting again. Even before the lightning has disappeared, they're counting. But they're counting into the void, so to speak.

BOOK REVIEW: In several sentences, you draw that phrase out repeatedly. I had the impression that you wanted to imitate the lightning chain syntactically with a chain of sentences.

WOLF HAAS: Really? What chain of sentences do you mean?

BOOK REVIEW: This really ungrammatical passage here. You write that "the lightning, which illuminated the night sky where it had not yet rained, as bright as day, but the thunder. As far as you could see, the landscape gleamed in this unnaturally bright light, but the thunder."
WOLF HAAS: Yes, okay.

BOOK REVIEW: "We walked, we ran, we panted, we stumbled, we rushed, we hurried, we trembled, we raced to the other side of the power lines, higher up the mountain, but the thunder."

WOLF HAAS: I know the passage you mean.

BOOK REVIEW: "We turned our heads toward the lingering lightning that had plunged all the hills and the whole valley and all the mountains and the entire sky into violent high-voltage light, but the thunder."

WOLF HAAS: But the thunder didn't come.

BOOK REVIEW: "But the thunder didn't come." And there you even start a new paragraph before you end the sentence.

WOLF HAAS: I like the fact that you read that passage as a reflection of the inextinguishable lightning. I don't think I thought about it though. I always wrestle with other things while I'm writing, mostly weight problems, you could say. The airplane's always too heavy to take off because I've loaded in too much informational baggage. It's overweight. So I see what else I can smuggle in there as a carry-on, or whom I offload something onto without his thinking I'm a terrorist, etc.

BOOK REVIEW: I won't let you distract me. I have the impression you aren't too comfortable with the "mystical moment" interpretation of your work.

WOLF HAAS: No, not at all. Maybe you're right. It's also really awesome when a whole landscape is encapsulated in a bright bubble of light for a second. You can almost get emotional about it. I just think it's a little overblown. In the final analysis, it's just a storm.

BOOK REVIEW: It's not just about the lightning that illuminates the whole mountain range as though it were day. And it's also not necessarily the absence of thunder that makes the two young lovers keep up this methodical counting into the void.

WOLF HAAS: For me, the thunder – or lack of it – is the most threatening part.

BOOK REVIEW: But, along with the thunder, the whole world disappears for a moment. I underlined this passage: "No lightning struck. It didn't thunder. Not a single drop of rain! The wind didn't blow. For a second it was so quiet because the crickets stopped chirping, the insects stopped buzzing, and the downpour hadn't started yet. It was so silent because even the power lines had stopped humming."

WOLF HAAS: It's crazy. Of course it's a little premature to say that the high tension wires had stopped humming. Logically, the noise stopped only a second later. That's for all those people who get their kicks scanning films for continuity errors.

BOOK REVIEW: Those seem to be your kind of people.

WOLF HAAS: Because it's logically wrong! On the same page it says that the only thing you could hear, very softly, were the storm alarm bells that suddenly echoed up from the village.

BOOK REVIEW: Yes, the storm bells. These are also very important for the mood at this moment. And you write literally "from the endless distance" one hears the storm bells. It almost sounds as if the sound of the bells comes from the heavens.

WOLF HAAS: It comes from the village church, though. If the high tension wires really weren't humming anymore, the bells couldn't ring. They run on electricity.

BOOK REVIEW: Well, no. For the reader it's completely beside the point. In this passage where everything stops, everything goes silent, the landscape is in a cone of light as if a UFO were landing right then – whether the wires went silent at that very moment or just a moment later doesn't really matter.

WOLF HAAS: It does matter!

BOOK REVIEW: I mean, nobody reads that logically to see if the infinitely distant church bells could ring if the high tension wires had stopped humming. Maybe the bells were connected to another power source.

WOLF HAAS: Yes, from the other side.

BOOK REVIEW: Or the sexton rang them by hand.

WOLF HAAS: That only happens in the Wild West.

BOOK REVIEW: Or the heavy bells swing back and forth a few times even though the power is already out. Or the sound is still traveling for a few seconds, taking its time creeping up the mountain at 340 meters per second or whatever.

WOLF HAAS: Right, per second.

BOOK REVIEW: If you're going to hold yourself to such strict rules, then the part about the air is considerably less plausible.

WOLF HAAS: What part about the air?

BOOK REVIEW: You write, everything is gone. No more thunder. No more wind. No rain. No buzzing of insects. And the whole thing culminates with no more air to breathe.

WOLF HAAS: Yeah, there's no air.

BOOK REVIEW: But you don't write that metaphorically or anything. Instead, it's stated very realistically. The air is gone. Of course, maybe on some level it makes you think back to his mother's asthma.

WOLF HAAS: No, the asthma was made up. Faked, actually.

BOOK REVIEW: By contrast, the realistic claims are emphasized by pseudo-scientific associations when you write, quote, "The alpine air that we greedily sucked in, breathless, the mountain air that feeds the healthy red blood cells that we intended to repay with the oxygen debt owed to them, the entire mass of good air just rolled into a ball and went away."

WOLF HAAS: How do you think it feels when a storm like that fast-forwards five seconds? It was two kilometers away, and then all of a sudden . . .

BOOK REVIEW: Of course, you can also take it as hyperbole –

WOLF HAAS: It's not hyperbole!

BOOK REVIEW: Let me just finish. You can also read

it – you always interrupt me right when I'm about to pay you a compliment. I think the parallel to the air mattress in the beginning is wonderful.

WOLF HAAS: Now I'm having a mystical moment too. Or, at least a power outage. I really don't know what you're talking about.

BOOK REVIEW: The way the air mattress sucked the air out of the car's interior during the drive down.

WOLF HAAS: Oh I get it. But there are a hundred pages in between. Although – that's actually great, what you said! At the beginning, the air mattress sucks all the air from the inside of the car, and now the storm is sucking the air from the landscape.

BOOK REVIEW: Right now I'm not sure if you're making fun of me or what.

WOLF HAAS: I just don't want to crown myself with your laurels. I really like the way that you put those things together. But maybe when you're writing you have to get yourself into a contrived kind of altered state – now we're back at the mystical moment. But let's leave that alone. Right now, I can't really believe that I didn't see it.

BOOK REVIEW: Mr. Haas, you aren't a naïve author. You like to play the dumb Austrian a little bit, but you really can't write about air mattresses that suck the air out of the interior of a car five pages back, and then pretend there's no connection when you take pages describing how, before the downpour finally comes, the air gets sucked out of the landscape. You don't describe that with just one sentence. The reader really feels the air is gone. You show how the two lovers stop and turn around a few meters beyond the high tension wires one last time before they make the steep climb and see the unfading light and –

WOLF HAAS: You always say “the lovers.” That word doesn’t appear once in the whole book.

BOOK REVIEW: And then you write about how everything goes silent and disappears, even the air that surrounds both of them – I won’t say the “lovers” because then you know what awaits the two of them, and that would be somehow contrived – that surrounds the *lovers.* And the text draws it out for a very, very long time – also recalling stylistically the somewhat overdone air mattress passage. I’ll read it aloud to you.

WOLF HAAS: No, I already know what you’re talking about.

BOOK REVIEW: “All of us and the valley and the mountains and the air that encases the world must have congealed and taken off to someplace far away, where the troposphere and the stratosphere meet in order to wind up and smack us. It was –”

WOLF HAAS: Yes, okay.

BOOK REVIEW: “It was as if the concentrated air out there had already blown off the lid that holds the stratosphere on the troposphere; as if it had already crossed the tropopause; as if it had already erupted into the stratosphere like a massive volcano so it could speed around the planet and sneak up from the other side to sweep us off the face of the earth.”

WOLF HAAS: Phew. Out of context, that's hard to take. I only used all that in preparation for the boxer image. That's how it is with me, I often write whole chapters just so that one particular line I'm building up to is well-motivated.

BOOK REVIEW: Why was there so much build up to the boxer analogy?

WOLF HAAS: Well, because it's an outrageous comparison. An appalling comparison, actually. Like something out of an essay-writing competition in school.

BOOK REVIEW: Did you ever enter one of those?

WOLF HAAS: Why, do they really exist?

BOOK REVIEW: You think it's awful to say that the air pulled itself back like a boxer's fist?

WOLF HAAS: Absolutely! Everything comes together for me there. The air pulled back like the fist of a sweaty boxer, only to snap back a moment later and sweep the two lovers right off the scene. That is –

BOOK REVIEW: Now you said "the lovers" yourself.

WOLF HAAS: – an awful image. That's why I have to embed it really well, so it at least works on some level.

BOOK REVIEW: Why didn't you just get rid of the boxer?

WOLF HAAS: Because I needed him for the drops of sweat. I couldn't just leave those out. I wouldn't have known how to do it otherwise. It's like that, when a storm makes this kind of leap. Five minutes ago it was a glorious summer day. Three minutes ago it got dark. One minute ago you thought it was going to rain, but it didn't. Thirty seconds ago you thought the storm would back down. Twenty seconds ago it got unbearably close. Ten seconds ago the temperature dropped into the cellar. One second ago the air disappeared.

BOOK REVIEW: Like a boxer pulling back his fist.

WOLF HAAS: Yes. I know that it sounds a little forced. But I didn't need the boxer for the punch. I needed him for the droplets. Because it didn't start raining just like that – that's not how it goes! It doesn't just start raining buckets. You know what the English say? It's coming down in sheets.

BOOK REVIEW: Sheets?

WOLF HAAS: Like bed linen. Sheets.

BOOK REVIEW: Oh, right. It's raining sheets.

WOLF HAAS: It's raining bed sheets. Sheets. Without any space in between, flat sheets of rain. Not planes of rain. Just one sheet. The sky is falling, as it were, which is why the air gets pushed so violently over the fields.

BOOK REVIEW: But you say that sheet rain doesn't happen just like that?

WOLF HAAS: Beforehand there was this moment. Air – gone. A drop in the temperature, as if the local morgue had thrown its doors open.

BOOK REVIEW: That's good! Open house at the

morgue. It's a shame you didn't write that in the book.

WOLF HAAS: No, Kowalski never would have said that.

BOOK REVIEW: Too bad. You really feel the drop in temperature when you imagine the door of a morgue swinging open.

WOLF HAAS: Right, the door to the big refrigerator. There's something about that kind of sudden drop in temperature. But it wasn't about that for me. It was about how the few delicate drops of rain fell all at once head-on, not from above. Not rain. It's not raining yet. But instead, the wind sprays these fine drops, as if some heavyweight gorilla is about to strike the death blow and, like a harbinger of destruction, a few drops of sweat hit his opponent in the face.

BOOK REVIEW: The two of them didn't really feel the blow at all.

WOLF HAAS: That's how it is with real blows.

BOOK REVIEW: And for the reader, it's basically like that too. You have this moment of inertia and, while the two of them are already somewhere else, you hesitate. In your reading, you're still waiting expectantly down there where the two of them passed under the high tension wires, where they catch their breath a few meters past the wires and watch the lightning.

WOLF HAAS: Yes, the long second before that.

BOOK REVIEW: There was no rain and no lightning and no thunder. And there wasn't any more humming either. The insects were gone too. It was absolutely still.

WOLF HAAS: Just the clanging of the yellow DANGER sign on the high tension tower carrying over the hills.

BOOK REVIEW: Dancing

WOLF HAAS: Pardon me?

BOOK REVIEW: In the book it says: “Only the yellow tin sign with the word ‘DANGER’ danced, rattling loudly over the hills.” I only say that because this image made such an impression on me.

WOLF HAAS: It says “danced”? Oh, right. I changed that around a lot: danced, floated, hopped. Normally I don’t give a hoot, but here it was suddenly very important to me. The movement of the tin sign that skips around high over the hills.

BOOK REVIEW: The way the lightning did before.

WOLF HAAS: But to be honest now, I would rather have written “floated” than “danced.” Rattling in itself has an element of hopping in it, the way that it sort of keeps banging over and over. I don’t know why, but that’s somehow my favorite passage in the whole book. I always have a passage that is my personal favorite, and nobody really understands why it’s exactly that part.

BOOK REVIEW: I thought the place with the lipstick on the cheek was your favorite part?

WOLF HAAS: (*laughs*) I meant the passage where he was kissed.

BOOK REVIEW: Two centimeters in a straight line from the outer corner of the eye?

WOLF HAAS: Yeah, that's my favorite part. Kiss-wise.

BOOK REVIEW: Oh, no. Then let's talk about your other favorite part.

WOLF HAAS: To be honest, I've got a lot of them.

BOOK REVIEW: I'm talking about the tin sign with the word "DANGER"! What is it that you like so much about this passage?

WOLF HAAS: The way the rattling carried over the fields like in an old Western, like a ghost town. For me that's got a particular vibe. And it still hadn't started raining. You only hear the rattling. Other than that, you don't hear anything.

BOOK REVIEW: You write: "Other than that, you don't hear anything. The electric tower just crumpled."

WOLF HAAS: (*laughs*)

BOOK REVIEW: "The electric tower just crumpled. And at the same moment, a yellow neon lamp flickered on in the black sky. And at same moment, if not a split second before the light, the thunder broke loose, and when the thunder sounds simultaneously, or a split second before the lightning, you're standing in the middle of a storm. And –"

WOLF HAAS: In retrospect I'm always annoyed when I write such long sentences.

BOOK REVIEW: "– you're standing in the middle of a storm. And at that moment, when we are shocked that it's not raining yet, if not a moment before we were shocked, if not since time immemorial, because it was impossible to imagine that there was ever a different landscape here, suddenly, at the spot where we had climbed up the hiking path, a wild torrent cascaded down the trail."

WOLF HAAS: Please don't read my book aloud to me.

BOOK REVIEW: Does it make you uncomfortable?

WOLF HAAS: The absurd thing about this mountain torrent, which washes them down to the high tension tower, is that it came before it was clear to the two of them that the gust of wind had already flung them fifty meters. Almost up to the cattle gate! The mountain stream that carries them back down to the electric tower re-establishes the order.

BOOK REVIEW: Yes. And right in this passage – almost as if you put in a footnote - you digress for half a page to talk about the cave accident when the reservoir collapsed in October 1963 and water poured into the mineshaft and washed the miners away.

WOLF HAAS: I think we'd better talk about that tomorrow. I'm pretty tired today. And besides, we're already finished with this part. The two of them run into the smuggler's den and take shelter.

BOOK REVIEW: I wonder what you'd do to a critic who summarized your book like that.

WOLF HAAS: Why? That's more or less what I write in the book anyway.

BOOK REVIEW: I agree with you, to the extent that it's astounding how abruptly this scene ends, if you think about the elaborate way you describe the whole afternoon. You barely devote a page to the actual scene that the whole novel really depends on.

WOLF HAAS: The pivotal scene. Well, I'm not really so –

BOOK REVIEW: Then I'll call it the key scene or plot point, for all I care, if you don't have a problem with those terms.

WOLF HAAS: I do understand what you mean by "actual scene." In a way, the whole novel wouldn't exist if Anni hadn't saved his life, but I think you can only describe those things tersely. What is there to dwell on? She saved his life because she stopped him from running down the mountain. That's one sentence. Instead of allowing him to run down the mountain to his death, she grabbed him by the hand and pulled him up. One more sentence. They seek shelter in the smuggler's den. Third sentence. Fourth sentence: They pull off their soaking wet clothes. Fifth and sixth sentence: Wet, naked bodies in the hay, which makes the hay smell fragrant. Of course that's a ridiculously kitschy situation, so I cut and I cut, and it's just as unbearable.

BOOK REVIEW: Why do you think it's kitschy? I didn't think it was kitschy at all! I'm sure your female readers love this passage.

WOLF HAAS: I don't know, that's a sort of indiscreet

question. Have you ever lain in hay?

BOOK REVIEW: Let's just say, I can imagine that it must be very romantic.

WOLF HAAS: Where did you get that idea?

BOOK REVIEW: I read your book!

WOLF HAAS: Oh that doesn't come across at all. You can't describe something like that. I got rid of all of it. I just left in the sentence that says the two, well, the two –

BOOK REVIEW: – Lovers.

WOLF HAAS: Yes, for all I care. That the two are lying *au naturel* in the hay shivering from cold, and the hay starts to give off this scent.

BOOK REVIEW: Like the tar Anni's dad used to cement the driveway.

WOLF HAAS: Not "cement." Asphalt! Cement doesn't have that smell. But fresh tar, that's really something. And the big steamrollers leave water droplets on the freshly rolled hot tar that's sizzling so poisonously somehow, and the water's shimmering on top of the fresh tar like oil. That's really a wonderful smell, I'll tell you, and when two soaking wet bodies are lying in hay –

BOOK REVIEW: In the book, though, you compare it to the droplets that bead up on soaking wet jeans. You write that the two of them throw their jeans in a heap on the floor.

WOLF HAAS: "Heap of jeans." I like that. Wet jeans

are such an awful mess. Particularly back when jeans were really thick, even in summer. And water beaded up on them in droplets. He remembered that.

BOOK REVIEW: Of the water from the steamrollers, which sizzled on the fresh tar, as you write, when Anni's father asphalted the driveway.

WOLF HAAS: I can't just write two wet, naked bodies in the hay. I would be arrested, and rightly so.

BOOK REVIEW: And who's supposed to arrest you for it?

WOLF HAAS: I didn't mean it that literally.

BOOK REVIEW: I got that. You mean the kitsch police would come get you or something? But you only write a single sentence about the good scent of the hay and that the scent reminds Vittorio of the smell of the poisonous tar Anni's father used on his driveway.

WOLF HAAS: The scent of hay. That reminds me. I have a great name for a men's cologne: "Satan." I think I could get rich off of that.

BOOK REVIEW: You should copyright that. But let's stay on the topic of the hay scent.

WOLF HAAS: Yes, the sixth sentence, wasn't it? The scent of hay. The hay scent. All I have to do is say it and I've already got it in my nose.

BOOK REVIEW: I hope you don't have hay fever.

WOLF HAAS: Okay, so, the hay sentence. Number six

or seven. Then the driving rain pounds so hard on the roof of the smuggler's den that Anni's afraid it's going to drill holes through the roof. Okay now, the fear sentence. She thinks it's hailing. Pellets the size of children's heads, that's what it sounds like. But it's just the rain!

BOOK REVIEW: The sheet rain.

WOLF HAAS: Exactly. Raining cats and dogs. Then another sentence about the ever-dropping temperature.

BOOK REVIEW: Open house at the morgue.

WOLF HAAS: The drop in temperature is emphasized only because, well, as a sort of reason why they have to keep each other warm. Then, I think, there's another sentence about the warlike thunderclaps and about the lighting bolts that project a grid of light and shadow into the hut through the slats.

BOOK REVIEW: And then there's the knocking.

WOLF HAAS: Right, the knocking. That was the most difficult passage for me. I don't know if I should have left the knocking out. But on the other hand, you can't leave everything out when you're writing. The whole thing about the weather had already gotten to me. That they also talk about "weather" underground.

BOOK REVIEW: That's where the artistry comes in?

WOLF HAAS: Maybe not yet. But over in Lengede, the trapped miners were washed away by a sudden torrent – "weather" under the ground.

BOOK REVIEW: And on *Place Your Bets* all Kowalski's questions were about "weather," which can also mean "violent storms."

WOLF HAAS: (*sighs*)

BOOK REVIEW: Even Gottschalk made a joke about weather/whether.

WOLF HAAS: Yes, there are always parallels and convergences as if the whole world were just one big piece of mystical chewing gum.

BOOK REVIEW: Mystical chewing gum – you could get rich on that too, maybe. Although – perhaps it would be more something for your Austrian colleague Ransmayr.

WOLF HAAS: (*laughs*) You said it, not me.

BOOK REVIEW: Or Raoul Schrott.

WOLF HAAS: At any rate. None of these parallels would have bothered me so much, but then there were the knocking signals. In the mines, the knocking signals are the stuff of legends. It's all about knocking signals. That's pure mythology, this famous "and then we heard the knocking signals on the tenth day" and so on.

BOOK REVIEW: And so then Anni's father comes to the hut and starts making knocking signals.

WOLF HAAS: Yes, he knocks on the door because it's barred from the inside. That's fine. That's still just normal door knocking. It only turns into real "knocking signals" when the two of them don't open. Now he is suddenly knocking for his life.

BOOK REVIEW: I thought that was very artfully done.

WOLF HAAS: All right. Actually I didn't need any fancy knocking. He's just knocking like crazy because he was caught in the storm, too. He's panicking! He has to save himself from the storm, and he finds that his own smuggler's den is locked. Well, the real den was, of course, down below, well hidden in the cellar in the cliff. But he couldn't even get in from the upper level.

BOOK REVIEW: The children barred the door from inside before they lay down naked in the hay. It isn't entirely clear whether they can really hear the knocking signals in all the noise of the storm.

WOLF HAAS: They hear the knocking signals! But they're lying there naked, hugging each other in the hay. They convince themselves that no one is knocking. It's just the storm. They whisper in each other's ears to calm themselves down.

BOOK REVIEW: And they don't open the door.

WOLF HAAS: And they don't open the door.

BOOK REVIEW: And the next day Mr. Bonati's corpse washes up at a hydroelectric dam twenty kilometers across the border.

WOLF HAAS: Exactly. You're right, that is somehow a core scene.

BOOK REVIEW: The Smuggler's Last Ride. From the high tension tower to a hydroelectric plant across the border.

WOLF HAAS: Fifty kilometers in a deluge. There's something to that.

BOOK REVIEW: More than the highway, in any case. The highway where the family from the Ruhr found themselves later that day.

WOLF HAAS: Naturally they got out of Farmach in a hurry. And that's why Vittorio didn't return for fifteen years.

BOOK REVIEW: But you don't give away the actual reason for their hasty departure until much later in the book.

WOLF HAAS: Yes, well. You can't give away everything right at the beginning of a book.

BOOK REVIEW: Otherwise it wouldn't be a movie, as your aunt always said.

WOLF HAAS: Besides, Vittorio Kowalski needed fifteen years to learn the truth.

Day Four

BOOK REVIEW: Mr. Haas, I had a little bit of a panic attack last night at the hotel when I realized how much I'm still missing. We still haven't talked about Mrs. Bachl.

WOLF HAAS: We could do that now.

BOOK REVIEW: I also have nothing about Mrs. Bonati, her attentive work at the bed-and-breakfast.

WOLF HAAS: I don't have a lot about that either. Except that she was annoyed by the constant truck repairs and oil changes that her husband used to do in the driveway of the bed-and-breakfast instead of in the garage.

BOOK REVIEW: I don't have any of that. And I don't have anything about the constant arguing between Vittorio's parents! I'm also missing Anni's father's smuggling runs, and the rivalry between the two fathers over mountain-climbing.

WOLF HAAS: But that was one-sided. Vittorio's father wanted Bonati to accept him unconditionally. Bonati was head of the mountain rescue team and naturally arrogant. He tried not to show it, though. At least when his wife scolded him about being so condescending.

BOOK REVIEW: And, above all, I don't have the interesting point that Kowalski senior now and then evened the score some other way.

WOLF HAAS: But that was only when he'd had something to drink. The man couldn't hold his liquor.

BOOK REVIEW: Even though he worked at a tavern.

WOLF HAAS: Yes, he ran his tavern, but he definitely didn't drink there. He was too serious to drink on the job. On vacation, at the most! And it usually went straight to his head, especially if he'd been in the mountains beforehand.

BOOK REVIEW: Yes, okay. Maybe the alcohol was the catalyst. But as far as content goes, his reproaches were absolutely legitimate.

WOLF HAAS: One thing led to another. If Kowalski senior flaunted his long line of mining ancestors, it was only to compensate for his inferiority complex in matters of mountain climbing. And after that, Bonati would flaunt his long line of smuggling ancestors. And then when he trotted out his Nazi uncles who had been party members from day one, and lugged weapons over the mountains from Germany in the thirties, that started a huge Nazi fight every time.

BOOK REVIEW: That is really the only situation in which Kowalski senior breaks out of his subordinate role. He would never kiss up to him. Instead, he bravely told the smuggler exactly what he thought of these ancestors.

WOLF HAAS: He wasn't about to let Bonati pass off his story about the old Nazis as some romantic little weapons smuggling yarn.

BOOK REVIEW: I thought it was great that the swaggering local didn't impress the obstinate guest with his "little yarn." It also embarrassed his wife.

WOLF HAAS: And the kids for sure. Both men always got pretty loud when they started on this topic of who were the bigger Nazis, the Germans or the Austrians, and on and on.

BOOK REVIEW: Real rednecks.

WOLF HAAS: When fathers get red in the face and broadcast their opinions, kids can't take it. On the other hand, their shame about their parents really brought the kids together.

BOOK REVIEW: Speaking of shame, sometime we have to get around to talking about Vittorio Kowalski's arrival in Farmach, otherwise we'll never get to the wedding. His arrival was also a bit embarrassing.

WOLF HAAS: I wouldn't really mind if we didn't get to the wedding. I have to throw in the towel because I can't explain all the Hollywood kitsch. But of course these things color reality, that's an old problem of writing. What do you do as an author with a reality you invent yourself – with cops who act like cops on television, and with brides who want to get married just like in the movies, without this reflecting on you as the writer?

BOOK REVIEW: So you want to be let off the hook?

WOLF HAAS: I'm just trying to help you stop panicking about the time.

BOOK REVIEW: Don't worry, we'll get to the wedding. All in good time. I just can't let you digress too much with every question, then we'll manage. I have my reasons for wanting to talk about the days between Vittorio's arrival in the vacation paradise of his childhood and Anni's wedding –

WOLF HAAS: It's not a vacation paradise in that sense. It's just nowheresville where you can do a little hiking. His parents originally went there just because it was cheap. Because of the contract Ruhr Coal Industries, Inc. had with the tourism bureau in Farmach. Although his father was the first one in his family who didn't work at Ruhr Coal Industries. That's why he had such a sentimental attachment to mining history and indoctrinated his son with heroic legends from the time he was little.

BOOK REVIEW: And the son eventually got into mine demolition, of all things.

WOLF HAAS: Luckily his father never lived to see that, and his mother didn't care.

BOOK REVIEW: It occurred to me that as soon as Vittorio Kowalski reached the hotel, you start another countdown. This method of counting down runs like a red thread through the whole book. First on the highway: so and so many more kilometers until the border; then the storm, another three thousand more meters, another two thousand eight hundred meters; and now, five more, then four more days until Anni's wedding.

WOLF HAAS: I just like counting. Counting is a kind of meditation for me. Counting calms you down. Writing makes me nervous somehow, everything is always going in so many directions at once. I don't have the mind for it. Things get too complex for me very quickly, in the same way that a tangled shoelace makes me crazy. Counting, on the other hand, that's like a doctor giving you a pill. Or yoga or something. Or some kind of physiotherapy where they say to you, stand up straight, and then as an author you can also say to a text, just stand up straight, just seven more seconds, six more, five more seconds.

BOOK REVIEW: The counting in your book is in no way calming! It just predicts an explosion!

WOLF HAAS: Yes, true. When you're about to detonate something, the counting is a matter of life and death. But in this passage, you don't yet know that's going to happen.

BOOK REVIEW: First the smaller catastrophes happen.

WOLF HAAS: Which, of course, are always experienced as big catastrophes.

BOOK REVIEW: He had just parked his car in the hotel lot when he realized that he had reserved a room in Lukki's hotel, of all places.

WOLF HAAS: He had made a point of booking a room in a place with a name that he didn't recognize. Wellness Hotel Schwalbenwandblick. In the old days, there hadn't been any real hotels in the village, only bed and breakfasts.

BOOK REVIEW: Like the Elizabeth Bed and Breakfast that Anni's parents owned.

WOLF HAAS: Exactly. So he automatically thought, a four-star wellness hotel, that's got to be new, he could safely book a room there.

BOOK REVIEW: The moment he sees the hotel in front

of him, Lukki comes to mind.

WOLF HAAS: Because the hotel stands on the very spot where Lukki's parents' inn used to be.

BOOK REVIEW: The Luckschmid Inn.

WOLF HAAS: Luckschmid. Yes, what a weird name, but I can't do anything about it.

BOOK REVIEW: I didn't have a problem with the name when I was reading. But I had a big problem with the sentence that went through his head as he was getting out of his car.

WOLF HAAS: "Oh, this fresh air!" Did it bother you that in his head he heard the hefty sigh that his mother always vented when she squeezed her way out of the car?

BOOK REVIEW: No, I don't mean that. I actually thought it was really nice, how he heard his long-dead mother sighing "Oh, this fresh air." But even before that, before he got out of the car. When he pulls into the parking lot and sees the hotel he gets this terrible sense of recognition that he expresses in the book: "Lukki, that bastard, I'd forgotten about him."

WOLF HAAS: That's too rough for you?

BOOK REVIEW: No. Too far-fetched. I can't believe he would completely forget his bitter rival over the years. That this – enemy, almost – just occurs to him now. Just when he realizes he's reserved a room in Lukki's hotel, of all places.

WOLF HAAS: Of course I had a problem with this too, but not because it was unbelievable. I think it's entirely believable. As I said, over the years all he had in his head was the weather. If he could barely remember Anni, why shouldn't he have completely repressed the memory of the idiot from next door?

BOOK REVIEW: So what's your problem?

WOLF HAAS: In a novel, you can't really introduce a new character halfway into the story. I tried to work him in earlier. I could have easily introduced Lukki during the arrival, when all the memories of those past summers come back to him.

BOOK REVIEW: Lukki, as the boy next door, was definitely part of those summer memories. Swimming pool, riding bikes, badminton –

WOLF HAAS: – getting beaten up, being held under water for minutes.

BOOK REVIEW: You don't forget things like that.

WOLF HAAS: Yes, as I said, I could have easily sneaked Lukki into the Kowalskis' random thoughts during their journey. Even if in reality he never thought about Lukki for even a second. Otherwise he never could have thought in front of the hotel, "Lukki, that bastard, I'd forgotten all about him."

BOOK REVIEW: And it seemed so important to you, to do justice to a sense of documentary reality?

WOLF HAAS: Just the opposite. I am no slave to truth. But the longer I fooled around with it, the clearer it was to me that the actual void in his memory creates the most interesting slant. Sort of against accepted literary technique.

BOOK REVIEW: But it's at the expense of credibility. As a reader you think to yourself, he can't possibly have forgotten Lukki completely.

WOLF HAAS: Forgotten, no. He just hadn't thought about him. That's different. And this business of popping up suddenly where he doesn't belong – what do you call these diabolical little heads that pop out of a box when you open the lid? Sort of a "devil ex machina," what are they called?

BOOK REVIEW: Jack-in-the-box?

WOLF HAAS: I don't know. Not jumping devils? Actually it's just a red devil's head and the body's the spring, and when you open the lid, it pops out.

BOOK REVIEW: That's the effect you were looking for? That Lukki suddenly jumps into the novel like a jack-in-the-box?

WOLF HAAS: Yes, or pops out of the book. I always have the feeling that things should pop out of the book. That's a feeling I have about writing. The paper is so flat, such a smooth surface, that once in a while something should reach out from the middle fold, or whatever you call it.

BOOK REVIEW: Or leap out.

WOLF HAAS: That's like Henry Rollins, how his first girlfriend always got red spots on her neck when they were having sex and he always used to pray to God that sometime these spots would appear in the form of a cross.

BOOK REVIEW: Henry Rollins prayed to God? And you're praying to the jack-in-the-box, or what?

WOLF HAAS: As a reader you just casually stick your nose in a book. And something should pop out, I always wish for those sorts of things when I write, that things really shoot off sparks.

BOOK REVIEW: But there aren't any sparks until Mr. Kowalski enters the hotel lobby, and the announcement grabs him.

WOLF HAAS: "Grabs" is good.

BOOK REVIEW: No jokes. In other words, this announcement that the hotel owner will be marrying Anni the next weekend.

WOLF HAAS: Yes, that's it. That pains me. I don't like to think about it, even today. After fifteen years he drives across half of Europe to the vacation spot of his childhood –

BOOK REVIEW: It's also a trip through time, driving down to the land of the past.

WOLF HAAS: – and then there's this notice in the lobby. It still pains me today to think about it. You appear on television and you make this romantic challenge with all your might; you get a card that your best friend forged; you drive down and then right on this notice, you read that the hotel restaurant will be closed the following weekend for the wedding.

BOOK REVIEW: That must have taken the wind out of his sails, because the night porter tried to calm him down by explaining that it applied to next weekend and wouldn't affect him.

WOLF HAAS: After the long drive he was naturally limp. He didn't have a lot of energy to fake it.

BOOK REVIEW: Strictly speaking he couldn't have known that it was Lukki of all people who would be taking Anni to the altar. According to your book, the notice only said the hotel restaurant would be closed for a day for the hotel manager's wedding. No names.

WOLF HAAS: Yes, two days.

BOOK REVIEW: But no names. And in fifteen years a lot can happen. Lukki could have fallen in love a hundred times with other women.

WOLF HAAS: Well, you don't know Anni.

BOOK REVIEW: That doesn't explain it for me. In fifteen years a lot can –

WOLF HAAS: But he knew it! You just know things like that.

BOOK REVIEW: You mean, he feels it.

WOLF HAAS: (*laughs*) Exactly, he feels it! Men feel things too, sometimes. Just like schnitzel.

BOOK REVIEW: Schnitzel?

WOLF HAAS: In the Vienna subway a few years ago there was a campaign about vegetarianism with all these posters about not eating meat. You saw a poor animal being led to slaughter and it said "Your schnitzel had feelings."

BOOK REVIEW: Disgusting!

WOLF HAAS: Well, and what if he didn't feel it –

BOOK REVIEW: With men, of course, it's not a "terror feeling."

WOLF HAAS: – then he would have found out the next morning at the latest when a radiant Anni floated into the breakfast room on Lukki's arm.

BOOK REVIEW: I've been wanting to get to this scene all along. Since that part about the jack-in-the-box.

WOLF HAAS: Or spring-devil, or whatever they're called. I always want to say devil-in-the-cake, but that's dumb.

BOOK REVIEW: The only thing that pops out of cakes is naked ladies.

WOLF HAAS: The devil of surprise. That sounds like a Peter Handke title.

BOOK REVIEW: Let me ask my question. You say that despite all of the misgivings it was the right thing for Lukki to suddenly pop up like the devil in the novel.

WOLF HAAS: Yes.

BOOK REVIEW: But you depict Lukki as being very likeable. Not at all like a devil. You get the impression that Lukki's a nice young man. Athletic, good looking, hotel owner. I imagined an Austrian ski instructor.

WOLF HAAS: Sure. He's likeable too. I can't put him in there as the villain because he stole Vittorio's summer love. As an Austrian I kind of have to side with Lukki. Besides his likeable entrance isn't necessarily a contradiction. The devil is always charming.

BOOK REVIEW: Okay, so is he a devil for you?

WOLF HAAS: No, he's not a devil for me at all. He didn't marry my wife.

BOOK REVIEW: I'd like to ask you more about that later.

WOLF HAAS: Let's drop this stupid "devil" expression right now. I never wanted to say that there was anything diabolical about Lukki. Even though it fits pretty well with his appearance: angular face, big nose, black eyes. By the way, in Austria we say that someone is "a handsome devil."

BOOK REVIEW: A good-looking man.

WOLF HAAS: Yes. Like a ski instructor type, or a mountain guide. He was a good match for Anni.

BOOK REVIEW: So what's it going to be? Devil or no devil?

WOLF HAAS: That's why I keep saying devil-in-the-cake. It's not about diabolical contents, it's about surprise. Suddenly he's there, and you can't get rid of him.

BOOK REVIEW: In your book you even say that Lukki would be the best proof for the theory that the worst kids become the nicest adults. What kind of theory is that? Does it really exist?

WOLF HAAS: No, I don't think so.

BOOK REVIEW: You just write something like that into your novel? Aren't you worried that people will take that seriously and it will be somehow incorporated into the body of common knowledge?

WOLF HAAS: I put that in more for my friends because they all have such spoiled kids. Loudmouthed and fresh. Obnoxious brats. And I thought to myself maybe they'd be happy to read that even the worst kids can become upstanding people. Lukki was a real jerk as a kid.

BOOK REVIEW: I don't want to step on your toes, but you almost show pleasure in listing all the things Lukki did to the punier vacation kid.

WOLF HAAS: Yeah, pooling.

BOOK REVIEW: Pooling?

WOLF HAAS: Isn't that how you say it? Pushing someone under water and holding him there and not letting him up for minutes.

BOOK REVIEW: A torturer. But a handsome devil.

WOLF HAAS: Kids are rough. And Vittorio had the

short end of the stick. I was barely able to resist suggesting that's why he may have been a little funny in the head. From frequent oxygen deprivation, when the bully held him underwater.

BOOK REVIEW: There's really a fiendish irony here. His mother wanted to come to the place for the good air, and her son was regularly deprived of it.

WOLF HAAS: Yes, but you're not saying that that has anything to do with the air mattress passage.

BOOK REVIEW: How dumb do you think I am, really? For me, this dunking means nothing more than physical brutality. Lukki is clearly proof that a bully can also grow up all right.

WOLF HAAS: To be honest it was more of a trick that I emphasized it so much. I needed the sentence about the brutal kids as preparation for the sentence about Anni.

BOOK REVIEW: Lukki is evidence that even the most brutal children can often become the nicest adults, and Anni is evidence that even the most beautiful women –

WOLF HAAS: Not the most beautiful women. Other way around. Anni is proof that the snottiest girls become the most beautiful women. I'm just in love with this stupid sentence. I heard it from Mrs. Bachl. The snottiest girls make the most beautiful women, she said and smiled off-handedly, when I was asking her about Anni's childhood.

BOOK REVIEW: Oh, we really have to talk about Mrs. Bachl!

WOLF HAAS: She said it in total seriousness. Out of her mouth it sounded like ancient wisdom, that the snottiest girls become the most beautiful women.

BOOK REVIEW: You're smiling.

WOLF HAAS: I can't say it without lapsing into a state of euphoria.

BOOK REVIEW: Mr. Haas, this folk wisdom that snottiest girls become the most beautiful women isn't all that meaningful for the reader. It's a nice proverb, maybe, and it makes you smirk, but in the book it's just one sentence out of many. Why is the statement so important to you?

WOLF HAAS: It all sounds so stupid now, but in reality they're very practical-minded thoughts. Just plain-thinking. Remember, I'm also an engineer.

BOOK REVIEW: I hope you're not going to say "text-engineer" or something so uptight and 1960s sounding.

WOLF HAAS: Well, yes. Text-engineer. Do you think that's so bad? That the snottiest girls become the most beautiful women is the only passage where I say something about Anni's beauty. There's nothing more difficult in a novel than a beautiful woman. It's hellish! It's embarrassing and banal.

BOOK REVIEW: Good that you say that.

WOLF HAAS: A beautiful woman always pops up somewhere in a novel. And then I'm always afraid when I'm reading aloud that all good-looking women in the audience are going to roll their eyes because they find it so silly when you mention these or those characteristics. Well, it's really, it's like – do you know what *Salzburger Dumplings* are?

BOOK REVIEW: I know Mozart balls. But not these.

WOLF HAAS: It's not really a dumpling, it's kind of dessert soufflé made of egg-white and sugar, in other words – do you also call it "snow" in Germany?

BOOK REVIEW: Egg-snow, yes.

WOLF HAAS: And they rise in the oven, and then you really have to be careful that the dumplings don't collapse when you serve them. And something like that happens when you describe a beautiful woman in a book: it's incredibly difficult to serve.

BOOK REVIEW: You can see that your father was a waiter.

WOLF HAAS: That's just common knowledge in a tourist country.

BOOK REVIEW: But Mr. Haas, it's already clear from the first line that it's going to be about a stunningly beautiful woman. It's in the way Kowalski looks at her. The look of desire.

WOLF HAAS: Although I never overtly write that! Except in the passage where old Mrs. Bachl says the snottiest girls become the most beautiful women.

BOOK REVIEW: Well, I wouldn't bet my life on it, but I do have the impression that you write how beautiful Anni is many times in the book.

WOLF HAAS: No, definitely not. I would have known. It makes me sick when I'm forced to describe a woman's beauty in a book. As an author you turn into a sweaty old horned toad sitting in front of your keyboard. But in this case it was more or less impossible to leave it out. And with Anni it was particularly difficult because I liked her, I mean personally.

BOOK REVIEW: You can tell.

WOLF HAAS: Why are you looking at me like that?

BOOK REVIEW: I'm hesitating because I'm not sure if I should say what's on the tip of my tongue.

WOLF HAAS: Which is?

BOOK REVIEW: I'm still stuck at your earlier choice of words "it makes one sick." It's like this, certain kinds of descriptions of women turn your stomach if you're a female reader.

WOLF HAAS: That's exactly why it's so important that I didn't write anywhere how beautiful Anni is, except for that part with the snot.

BOOK REVIEW: I'm not saying that you don't write about it cleverly. I just don't know if that changes a lot about your perception. One doesn't learn a lot about Anni herself from the book. It's more about Vittorio's obsession, while Anni has long ago evaporated into the clouds.

WOLF HAAS: But that's the theme of the story! That's why I describe his entrance into the hotel lobby as a little bit unreal, a bit like a drug high. Because for the first time in fifteen years he's marching toward reality.

BOOK REVIEW: By the way, I almost expected that in this passage where he's floating through the hotel lobby toward the reception desk in this strange drug-like haze, I almost expected Anni to be standing there as the receptionist behind the counter. Sort of like out of a cake.

WOLF HAAS: Basically, that would have been better.

BOOK REVIEW: No, I don't think so. It's good as it is, that he sees her the next morning at breakfast. The expectation was just there because of the detailed way you described his walk through the lobby. Almost as in super slow motion.

WOLF HAAS: After a long drive in the car when you get out with this feeling in your legs and then go into a hotel lobby, there's something very Magic Mountainish about that. Maybe it just got to be so detailed because I wrote this scene while I was on a book tour. You always get hotel fever.

BOOK REVIEW: Yes, it's also some kind of roll of thunder that you describe there.

WOLF HAAS: You think so?

BOOK REVIEW: Behind his back the banging of the swinging door gets louder instead of softer. And the swinging door to his left, which leads from the hotel lobby to the dining room is banging too. And the rhythms of the doors overlap as they bang faster, the closer they come to stopping. You could also take that as knocking signals. When you know the ending, you can say that at the moment when he enters Lukki's hotel bad luck is already knocking.

WOLF HAAS: Well, but in the sense of "knocking" the way misfortune knocks, swinging doors don't do that. It's more of a knocking sort of flutter.With these swinging doors, for me it was more about the transitoriness, the crossroads-like quality of a hotel lobby. In the whole novel, everybody's always under way. But not heroically, like in a road movie, with the car radio blasting, but in a magnetic kind of back and forth.

BOOK REVIEW: Like the smallest building blocks of reality.

WOLF HAAS: No one is ever reliably there in a place or a passage, so to speak. That's also true of the ancestors. The daily journey to the underground mine shafts. Or on Anni's side, the mountain men, the smugglers. Everyone's always on the way somewhere.

BOOK REVIEW: To the "other" side?

WOLF HAAS: Where? Yes, exactly. (*Laughs*) To the other world.

BOOK REVIEW: You even summarized your novel like this in an interview: it's the story of two regions. One where people are always going up the mountains, and the other where people are always going into them.

WOLF HAAS: I really regretted this comment because, to me, it's been completely psychoanalytically misinterpreted. You know, people who penetrate mountains, and people who storm the peaks, or whatever.

BOOK REVIEW: In light of the orgiastic story that this is all leading up to, it's no wonder, right?

WOLF HAAS: As an author, you really have to watch out that you don't interpret your story to death.

BOOK REVIEW: The part where you devote so much space to his first trip through the hotel lobby, before he reads the notice, reads something like a quotation from Andy Warhol's diary. It said something like hotel lobbies are the most beautiful places, and who doesn't really want to spend the night in one?

WOLF HAAS: In the lobby of Lukki's Wellness Hotel *Schwalbenwandblick* he really wanted to escape. It was a rustic nightmare. That kind of yodel architecture is really insane.

BOOK REVIEW: It doesn't come across that crassly in the book.

WOLF HAAS: You can't use that in a novel. You can't have a building like that standing around in a book.

BOOK REVIEW: In one of your Detective Brenner novels, you probably would have written: Amnesty International should take care of it.

WOLF HAAS: Just about. But I got rid of everything, the decoration, the whole natural wood shit, I got rid of all of it. Originally I had a whole chapter where Mr. Kowalski can't fall asleep the first night, and in order to fall asleep, the demolition engineer comes up with an exact plan in his head of how all the hotel props can be disposed of in a cheap, environmentally friendly, way as quickly as possible.

BOOK REVIEW: Oh, now you go straight to the breakfast scene.

WOLF HAAS: Yes. Despite his sleeplessness he built up a little bit of hope during the night. He sits at breakfast and hopes that Lukki's bride maybe isn't Anni after all.

BOOK REVIEW: And the reader hangs on to this hope until the very end! Just because Kowalski is so sure, when you're reading you hope for some surprising turn of events, just to find that the author has been leading you around by the nose.

WOLF HAAS: I have to admit, that's what I was hoping as I wrote. But surprising turns of events aren't really my strong suit.

BOOK REVIEW: The way he sits at breakfast and meditates on the vacation vocabulary of his distant past – Austrian words for local rolls and apricot jam –

WOLF HAAS: Because just now he's eating a roll with apricot jam for breakfast.

BOOK REVIEW: – when you're reading, you hope that his negative expectations won't be fulfilled. You hope that just maybe Lukki will come in and tell him, okay, now to put it bluntly –

WOLF HAAS: – and tell him that Anni went away fifteen years ago with a broken heart and became a nun.

BOOK REVIEW: Exactly. We readers are pretty dumb! You just wish that she's still as hung up on the whole affair as he is.

WOLF HAAS: That she's the old maid next door dreaming of him and waiting for his return.

BOOK REVIEW: Mr. Haas, I could make it very easy for myself right now and say: you obviously don't dare let a woman have a reaction other than to beat a sorrowful retreat to a cloister or become an old maid.

WOLF HAAS: Just a minute! That's not fair. You're twisting my words. I was just joking about options that were out of the question. That is the simplest trick of debating: taking the most obviously ironic statement literally.

BOOK REVIEW: The polemicizing, even if it's not so terribly simple-minded, Mr. Haas, could be seen from your point of view, if you were to guide the conversation to a point where cloisters and spinsterhood were the only conceivable alternatives to Anni's status as a happy bride.

WOLF HAAS: Fine. You force me into it. But please don't say afterwards that I took you for stupid just because I explained.

BOOK REVIEW: You have to leave what I say up to me.

WOLF HAAS: Okay. Point one, Anni and Lukki float radiantly arm in arm into the breakfast room to greet their childhood friend.

BOOK REVIEW: That's really how it was.

WOLF HAAS: Right. Point two, you just said that the reader hopes until the last minute that it will be different. That it's only Lukki who comes in and tells him something. That's where I interrupted you. Now I ask you, what do you hope that Lukki tells him?

BOOK REVIEW: Well, something about Anni. Something better than that Lukki is marrying her, but not as "clichéd" as a cloister or old maid.

WOLF HAAS: Okay. Point three.

BOOK REVIEW: You really do like counting!

WOLF HAAS: You can tell that my comments about "cloisters" and "old maids" are just caricatures, because they're alternatives that you'd find in a biography of a woman living in the 19th century, but in Central Europe in the 21st century –

BOOK REVIEW: Clearly. The whole point of my objection is that you're using these "caricatures" to disguise the realistic versions where a woman in the 21st century regrets the failure of her young love, maybe even grieves for it, without its reaching the level of caricature. That's exactly how it seems in Anni's case! You even write yourself that she was very sad the night after Vittorio's appearance on *Place Your Bets.*

WOLF HAAS: Point four: my caricature about using the cloister and old maid should therefore be understood as a comment about readers' expectations. Everyone knows that, in contrast to women's biographies, everything that relates to literature is really stuck in the 19th century.

BOOK REVIEW: But enough about polemics!

WOLF HAAS: Which is why, as soon as people start reading a story, they check their intellect at the door and just want the protagonists to end up together. You don't want to think about whether Anni might be better off with the hotel owner. You identify with Vittorio.

BOOK REVIEW: Well, I identified with Anni.

WOLF HAAS: Point five – okay, with Anni then. Point five. You identified with Anni, but definitely not with Lukki. I forgot the fifth point.

BOOK REVIEW: By the way, you didn't have to justify it in such detail. You interrupted me and I didn't finish my sentence that started with "to put it bluntly" about what Lukki could have said about Anni in the breakfast room. But now let's cut the bluntness and be serious. Of course I hoped that they would end up together. That's kind of why people read stories like this.

WOLF HAAS: I'm sure you know the saying, "The metaphor is smarter than its author."

BOOK REVIEW: Lichtenberg. That's actually a pretty clever aphorism.

WOLF HAAS: It only tells half the truth, though. The metaphor is not only smarter than its author, it's also smarter than its reader.

BOOK REVIEW: Are you calling me stupid!

WOLF HAAS: Well, I…that's a joke, right?

BOOK REVIEW: Lightning wit, eh? But back to the

topic. I think it's very telling that our conversation has drifted so far from the text in this painful passage where Anni and Lukki stroll so happily into the breakfast room.

WOLF HAAS: It hurt me most of all.

BOOK REVIEW: So you checked your intellect at the door too?

WOLF HAAS: These sorts of judgments aren't fair. Lukki was actually very sweet to him. He read the names on the guest list in the morning and then he went looking for him right away. They were really happy about the prominent visitor who made their little village famous. Of course, for a hotel owner, free advertisement on the television is a gift from heaven.

BOOK REVIEW: Anni was a lot more ambivalent.

WOLF HAAS: Not that bad really. Paradoxically, the sleepless night after the television debut helped her reach closure with the whole story.

BOOK REVIEW: A kind of delayed grieving.

WOLF HAAS: She had to face the whole situation, and inwardly say goodbye to him. Well, I believe it would have irritated her more if he had just appeared in the hotel without having been on TV beforehand.

BOOK REVIEW: That also explains why she appears like a radiant bride when she enters the breakfast room on Lukki's arm.

WOLF HAAS: That's not quite the way it is, except maybe on the outside. And she's really glad to see

Vittorio. She's also beaming because she sees him again.

BOOK REVIEW: This is one of the few passages in the book where your narrator briefly loses his friendly, painfully positive view of things. You have him say he sat like an idiot in the breakfast room of Lukki's luxury hotel as the radiant couple literally "surrounded" him.

WOLF HAAS: Yes, surrounded, I like that too. Speaking literally, two people can't surround someone, but when you're sitting, and a radiant couple is suddenly standing in front of you –

BOOK REVIEW: and you're in love with the bride –

WOLF HAAS: – you can definitely feel surrounded.

BOOK REVIEW: Hence his incredible greeting.

WOLF HAAS: "This is outrageous! " He himself didn't find that so outrageous. He felt like biting off his own tongue off after it slipped out.

BOOK REVIEW: I think it's great, the way he blurts it.

WOLF HAAS: But it was terribly embarrassing for him.

BOOK REVIEW: I was surprised he could be so quick-witted.

WOLF HAAS: It was something you'd sooner expect from Riemer. Snappy comebacks are a main subject in the curriculum of *Women for Dummies*. And especially in *Advanced Women for Dummies*.

BOOK REVIEW: This isn't the first time the sentence

"This is outrageous!" appears in the book.

WOLF HAAS: That comes from a very specific social milieu, or whatever you call it. "This is outrageous" was a phrase her parents liked to use when they felt cheated. When someone cut in front of them in line at the checkout, or a sale item came up full price at the register. Or at a restaurant when the people at the next table got their food first, even though they'd arrived later. And, for example, when it came to those arguments about old Nazis, both fathers used to yell it at each other.

BOOK REVIEW: "That's outrageous!"

WOLF HAAS: I really emphasized the outrage because at some point it occurred to me that in our society there is a kind of sociological dividing line. Sort of the "Fairness/Outrage" line. Self-confident people can be magnanimous and say something is unfair, but the frustrated underprivileged will snap, "Outrageous!"

BOOK REVIEW: You have to have a little bit of composure.

WOLF HAAS: And these escalating situations were always embarrassing for the kids. When their parents got worked up over some ridiculous thing. I just mentioned that because it was something Vittorio and Anni had in common from childhood. They were ashamed for their parents.

BOOK REVIEW: Blustering about outrage didn't suit Vittorio as an adult at all. He had risen to the milieu where one says "unfair."

WOLF HAAS: Exactly, that's why Anni and Lukki took

it ironically!

BOOK REVIEW: Didn't take it literally. Exactly the opposite, like the way simpleminded debaters take sarcastic comments literally. Just a while ago, you said it was unfair when I did that.

WOLF HAAS: I don't care. In any case, Vittorio had rarely been as serious about anything in his life. He thought it was incredibly outrageous that Lukki got Anni.

BOOK REVIEW: That's what makes it so painful. That he's not even taken seriously.

WOLF HAAS: He almost explodes with sorrow. Or, what am I saying, "almost explodes" – that's blown out of proportion –

BOOK REVIEW: I don't think it's blown too much out of proportion. That's exactly how it comes across in the book. It says "The wedding couple beamed at me from their four eyes so brightly that my ears started ringing. Ringing is okay," he says. So, his control of the ringing in his ears refers to the adult education course about not blushing, where he learned this method –

WOLF HAAS: The Mergan Method.

BOOK REVIEW: Where he learned this method to stop the cheeks from flushing. I didn't think this method of controlling blushing was all that great, by the way.

WOLF HAAS: But I need it here.

BOOK REVIEW: Uh huh. In this passage it's impressive how he conquers his blushing with this –

WOLF HAAS: Mergan Method.

BOOK REVIEW: But otherwise all the courses got on my nerves. Riemer and his *Women for Dummies* and the Italian course. I didn't need the additional course on how to stop blushing.

WOLF HAAS: That got on your nerves?

BOOK REVIEW: In places. A little.

WOLF HAAS: If things get on your nerves so easily, maybe you should take a course in autogenic training.

BOOK REVIEW: Very funny. But here, I concede that you do feel the enormous pressure he's under when he says ringing ears are okay. Because ringing is different from red and glowing.

WOLF HAAS: He believes that it's why the "outrageous" just slipped out.

BOOK REVIEW: Because he tried to halt the blush below the neuralgic border at the jaw bone.

WOLF HAAS: Exactly. Because at the mouth level it hit a sort of emotional traffic jam. He meant to say something to them as casually as possible. He struggled to come up with a cool remark like, I thought as much when I read the notice at the reception desk yesterday. But he couldn't think of anything.

BOOK REVIEW: He doesn't say he couldn't think of anything. It says, "But somehow the blood that was rushing to my head must have washed the wrong sentence over my lips because I didn't let it get any higher than the peach fuzz on the bottom part of my earlobe, in other words, just to mouth level. So, over the whirring and beating in my ears I heard myself saying loud and clear, almost screaming: This is outrageous!

WOLF HAAS: And both of them dissolve in laughter, because they think it's irony. Lukki skilfully takes the bait and repeats it, laughing, "Outrageous! That's what everybody's saying!" And he shakes his hand enthusiastically and keeps on joking: "But only one guy can marry her!"

BOOK REVIEW: I think it's very interesting that here you immediately switch levels from the dialogue to the overwhelming physical presence of Anni and Lukki.

WOLF HAAS: You mean the hugs?

BOOK REVIEW: You emphasize that Lukki was a head taller than Anni's father, who was himself a head taller than Vittorio's father.

WOLF HAAS: That was just because it's better for pit men to be smaller. Sort of a Darwinism of the mines.

BOOK REVIEW: And when Anni hugs him he finds her scent literally "better than a forest and a gas station put together."

WOLF HAAS: There's no deeper meaning there. They hug each other. When you get hugged, it feels like a giant is bending over you.

BOOK REVIEW: Or you feel that a woman smells

better than a forest and a gas station put together.

WOLF HAAS: Because that evening he'd filled up his gas tank thirty kilometers outside of Farmach. There really is a gas station right in the middle of the forest there. And that's where he noticed this bewitching scent, this mix of forest smells and toxic gas station fumes.

BOOK REVIEW: Bewitching industrial fumes come up a lot in this novel. The hay that smells like the fresh tar that Anni's father used when he poured the concrete on the driveway.

WOLF HAAS: Asphalt! I probably have a weakness for these smells because I worked at a gas station as a kid. The same way that Vittorio's brain was damaged by the repeated oxygen deprivation when he was held underwater in the swimming pool, mine was damaged by gas fumes. I felt sick the first day, but on the second day I thought it was pretty good. And on the third day I put my nose closer up to the tank. In those days there were no self-service gas stations, and you could earn money as a gas station attendant. And the rest I stole from Faulkner.

BOOK REVIEW: What did you steal from Faulkner? Have I missed something here?

WOLF HAAS: I really loved those places where it says "Caddy smelled like trees," and that's why Anni smells like the woods. But I put in the gas station part.

BOOK REVIEW: It's interesting, the first thing Anni says to him is, "You look great."

WOLF HAAS: That's just a thing you say when you

haven't seen somebody in a long time: "You look great."

BOOK REVIEW: And Lukki says, "Hey, we saw you on TV!"

WOLF HAAS: You notice the "hey." You look good, hey, we saw you on TV. A sneaky, hidden reason: he suddenly looks better because they saw him on television.

BOOK REVIEW: That interpretation seems a little harsh to me. When you're reading it, you get the impression that they're both pleased to see their old vacation pal again, whom they also happened to see on TV.

WOLF HAAS: Sure. Lukki was thoroughly naive in this situation. He didn't mean anything unkind, you're right. Such self-confident people aren't that suspicious. That's why Lukki never connected the television appearance with Anni. At this point he became effusive, clapped his hand on Vittorio's shoulder, and complimented him on his TV appearance.

BOOK REVIEW: Really awful

WOLF HAAS: You think that's so awful?

BOOK REVIEW: It's painful the way Lukki congratulates him when he's incredibly disappointed, with that deflating, "you were so great!"

WOLF HAAS: "Hey, dude, that was like so great. Really great."

BOOK REVIEW: Give me a break! When I read it, it was almost too much. You really feel for Vittorio.

WOLF HAAS: That's the whole point.

BOOK REVIEW: But he's so belittled here, it's unbearable. As a single person you can commiserate with what it's like to be with such a publicly happy couple. That's really hard to take, even when you're just in their presence, but even more when the poor guy's in love with Anni.

WOLF HAAS: On the other hand, you get it, that they were both incredibly nice to him. They gave him a warm welcome. I mean, their welcome was friendlier than in all those years when he was just a summer kid. They could have ignored him completely.

BOOK REVIEW: I was amazed that he didn't just leave right then. In that situation I would have packed my bags immediately.

WOLF HAAS: He wanted to stay for the two nights he'd booked so he wouldn't look stupid. On no account for the wedding. Of course they invited him to it right away and even offered him a free room.

BOOK REVIEW: And then in the evening there was the big mess with the wedding dress.

WOLF HAAS: Well, it wasn't a huge mess, just a humiliation.

BOOK REVIEW: In any case, that was the decisive meeting between the two of them.

WOLF HAAS: It was certainly a low blow that Anni invited him to her bedroom to see her in her wedding dress while Lukki was away in his jeep. Because the groom's not supposed to see it, but she could show it to Vittorio.

BOOK REVIEW: As though he were a girlfriend or something.

WOLF HAAS: Exactly.

BOOK REVIEW: It was far from charming the way she said it to him, "You're not allowed to show it to the groom. That's bad luck. But I can show it to you!"

WOLF HAAS: I would have shot myself then and there.

BOOK REVIEW: Well it was appropriate that you experience the whole thing from Anni's perspective. Maybe she even did it on purpose. Just to send a clear signal. It's pretty pushy when someone makes such a bombastic declaration of love on TV.

WOLF HAAS: Well, I'm saying that I think that sort of helped her. Although – you can't call his TV appearance bombastic. He was much too discreet for that. It would have been bombastic if he had mentioned her.

BOOK REVIEW: And there he is, standing in the doorway. She just wanted him to believe, or, really accept, that she was marrying someone else. It wasn't easy for her either.

WOLF HAAS: I think she was perfectly aware of what she was doing. I mean, she just wanted clear boundaries.

BOOK REVIEW: That's probably why she said it so emphatically, "But I can show it to you." Psychologically speaking, she's setting really healthy limits.

WOLF HAAS: You can't blame her for pushing him away. But that she does it so seductively, to put it mildly, is just –

BOOK REVIEW: – a little cruel. At least the way it's presented in the novel.

WOLF HAAS: So now it's my fault?

BOOK REVIEW: Besides, I think this little impropriety fleshes out Anni's character. Makes her real. She's got her faults too. I have to say, I really like Anni, despite this monkey business with the wedding dress in the bedroom.

WOLF HAAS: There, you see! Me, too! And I wrote the bit with the wedding dress especially so that this limit-setting you talked about, as if it has just occurred to you in conversation –

BOOK REVIEW: No, that comes through in the book, but –

WOLF HAAS: But that's the whole point of this passage. It's clear that she was under pressure. Why are you always saying there isn't enough of Anni's point of view in the book?

BOOK REVIEW: I would have liked to find out more about her. In some passages she comes across as flat.

WOLF HAAS: So I should write that Anni is really good at sorting recyclables or something?

BOOK REVIEW: Why not? If it tells something about her.

WOLF HAAS: That doesn't work, though. You can't tell everything about a person and still make them appealing. People are appealing because you don't know too much about them.

BOOK REVIEW: But you gave a lot of space to her somewhat blatant method of setting limits, by showing him her wedding dress.

WOLF HAAS: She could have sent him home if she wanted to set limits. That would have been more humane.

BOOK REVIEW: But her cruelty shows that she isn't as neutral as she pretends. Feelings just aren't that clear-cut – not in people, not in women.

WOLF HAAS: What's that supposed to mean?

BOOK REVIEW: Because you said a little while ago that you can't know too much about people and expect them to be appealing.

WOLF HAAS: That's too deep for me. I compressed the whole fashion show to a minimum. The whole how-does-it-look-on-me, the whole or-do-you-think-the-skirt's-too-short, the whole and-there's-also-a-hat-and-veil-but-that-hasn't-been-delivered-yet, and that wasn't the half of it. She even tormented him with the whole rest of the wedding shit. She explained everything to him down to the smallest detail, a thousand wedding customs, flowers, menu, priest.

BOOK REVIEW: Something old, something new, something borrowed, something blue.

WOLF HAAS: The whole shebang! And naturally, again and again, "Do you think the weather will hold for the wedding?"

BOOK REVIEW: It's a shame that in a printed interview no one can hear you mimicking Anni's voice. In your novel it doesn't come across how much the whole thing with the wedding dress turns you off.

WOLF HAAS: Then people would have blamed me for being too uptight. I would have only written how beautiful the dress was, how great it looked on her.

BOOK REVIEW: This shorthand technique didn't seem to be a problem for you.

WOLF HAAS: She really looked stunning in it. It was a kind of vanilla-colored material, well, actually not vanilla, but more of a –

BOOK REVIEW: Yes, all right. It's nothing new; the author is fascinated with Anni's looks.

WOLF HAAS: Vanilla is almost more of a taste association. Maybe you know this line, it's from a song – *she really is a dish.* But, as a color it was more like –

BOOK REVIEW: Cut, Mr. Haas! I'd like to jump very abruptly to the next day. Kowalski's walk to the crumbling smuggler's den.

WOLF HAAS: Okay. But before he went up to the smuggler's den, he stopped by to see Mrs. Bachl. She was sitting on her red bench when he walked by her house. Where she always sits.

BOOK REVIEW: I want to talk about Mrs. Bachl separately. For me, she's really the best character in the novel.

WOLF HAAS: And also very important for his behavior later. I really think that if he hadn't talked to Mrs. Bachl, he wouldn't have gone up to the smuggler's den at all. He would have felt resigned and powerless, somehow. And instead of going up there, he would have probably left that morning.

BOOK REVIEW: I don't want to talk about Mrs. Bachl yet.

WOLF HAAS: Okay.

BOOK REVIEW: Three days and 23 hours before the wedding, Kowalski drives to the mountain climbers' parking place, leaves his car there, and hikes up to the smuggler's den in a light drizzle.

WOLF HAAS: He had always insisted that all he wanted to do was take a quick look at it from outside. But the fact that he takes the lamp from the toolbox in the car is evidence to the contrary.

BOOK REVIEW: Was it really a headlamp? I have to say, that sounds far-fetched. I mean, normally you just have a flashlight in your toolbox, if that.

WOLF HAAS: That was typical of his father. He gave it to him when he got his first car. I also wondered if I should leave it out because it seemed artificial. But it's also much more practical for changing a tire at night.

BOOK REVIEW: He stops and rests at each of the three benches; he passes under the high tension wires; and he's up at the top in an hour.

WOLF HAAS: It took him longer than that. Don't forget, romantic people walk slowly.

BOOK REVIEW: The door to the hayloft opens easily. But when he gets as far as the ruined secret entrance to the cellar, the rotten beams collapse under his weight, and he's trapped in the smuggler's cellar.

WOLF HAAS: It can happen that quickly.

BOOK REVIEW: "It can happen that quickly" is also one of those sentences that crops up a few times in your book.

WOLF HAAS: Well, if I have to be precise, then it actually means something quite different. "It can happen quickly" is something Mrs. Bachl says about the weather. To comfort him. Or to give him a glimmer of hope that the rain could pass by before Anni's wedding. That's why she emphasizes it. Beautiful wedding weather can happen overnight. In this sense, "it can happen quickly." On the other hand, there is this existential experience of how quickly *it* can happen, the way a budding life can quickly end, which is, of course, something that wouldn't frighten somebody like Mrs. Bachl anymore.

BOOK REVIEW: Because she's been out there sitting on her red bench since the creation of the world.

WOLF HAAS: Exactly. By the way, when Anni was a little girl, she really believed it because her father never missed a chance to say that: old Mrs. Bachl has been sitting on her red bench watching the weather since the creation of the world.

BOOK REVIEW: Vittorio Kowalski's mood, on the other hand, is more end-of-the world, once he realizes the mess he's in.

WOLF HAAS: He realizes right away that he's buried. Because the dirt poured into the passageway behind him. He wasn't unconscious, not even dazed. He landed softly because of the mattresses on the floor, and he knew that nobody was going to come looking for him up there.

BOOK REVIEW: And no cell phone reception in that cellar dug deep in the mountain.

WOLF HAAS: Wouldn't have been any. He was deep in the mountain. But in little details like this he's more like his petty-minded father than he would like to admit. For example, he had made it a matter of principle never to take his cell phone with him on vacation.

BOOK REVIEW: The joke is that someone from the Ruhr mining region would get buried in the Alps, of all places.

WOLF HAAS: Yes, well. I don't want to explain the humor in my book. But the joke is also that his profession in the Ruhr involves calming down hysterical people.

BOOK REVIEW: I thought the "Operation Groundless Citizens' Initiative" was a pretty wicked caricature.

WOLF HAAS: I had no choice. I had to describe them from Kowalski's point of view. And anyway it was his job to keep them in check. Naturally it wasn't a pure love relationship.

BOOK REVIEW: And now he himself is buried in a ludicrous cellar built into a cliff. And in much greater danger than any buried miner because nobody is looking for him.

WOLF HAAS: Nobody had any idea where he was. Stupidly enough, he drove away from the hotel, so people there must have thought he'd left town. They had no idea he'd gone up the mountain.

BOOK REVIEW: And Lukki was captain of the mountain rescue team. Just like Anni's father.

WOLF HAAS: Of course, they would have pulled him out of there immediately. But they had no idea.

BOOK REVIEW: On the other hand, Vittorio knew perfectly well that you couldn't see anything from the outside.

WOLF HAAS: Basically, not much happened. The rotten cellar stairway collapsed under him and the dirt poured in and blocked the exit. It was a kind of half-excavated cellar in the rock underneath the hayloft. An ancient smuggler's den built over a crevasse in the cliff. Well, cliff wall, it was only walled in on one side. But poorly, and it hadn't been repaired in years. And that's where the dirt poured in.

BOOK REVIEW: In any case, the blockage was so

massive that he didn't even try to dig his way out.

WOLF HAAS: It was hopeless. With his bare hands! He couldn't have done it with a shovel. You couldn't see anything from above. But from his vantage point it was –

BOOK REVIEW: – as though he were trapped in Aladdin's Cave.

WOLF HAAS: Which had just been sealed for all eternity. And there was certainly no shovel there. On the other hand, the storeroom was a hoard of countless smuggled objects, but not a shovel among them. You have to say he was lucky, or more dirt would have poured in behind him and buried him alive. Or he would have weakened himself with so much exertion that he would have died of exhaustion the next day.

BOOK REVIEW: Terrible!

WOLF HAAS: Yes, when I wrote this passage I was sweating blood. To make it not read like *Five Friends and the Old Smuggler's Den* or something.

BOOK REVIEW: Yes, well. You really do everything so it doesn't come across that way. You devote pages to all the objects that he finds in the storeroom.

WOLF HAAS: Naturally there was a pile of stuff there because nobody had entered the storeroom since Anni's father died.

BOOK REVIEW: You even give an inventory of all of the moldering old junk that had been sitting there for fifteen years. Crummy old tape decks, coffee makers, wheel rims, mixers, microwaves, lamps, tools, record players, pots, pans, typewriters.

WOLF HAAS: It really is bizarre, to be buried with all this plunder.

BOOK REVIEW: Modern funerary offerings.

WOLF HAAS: Modern funerary offerings, I like that. I didn't make that association at all. For me it was more symbols of prosperity from bygone days, well, just old appliances that had outlived their usefulness.

BOOK REVIEW: In your book you say that the appliances don't look like they'd been there for only fifteen years.

WOLF HAAS: Rather, since Mrs. Bachl's birth. Which, we all know, was a very long time ago.

BOOK REVIEW: The smuggler who died in an accident fifteen years ago is still very present here thanks to all these objects. It's as though his avenging spirit had taken the form of these bizarre appliances to escort this man to his death. If you wanted to overdramatize it, you could say that Vittorio took his daughter and his life, but now the truck driver returns, in the form of this contraband and –

WOLF HAAS: Hmm . . . "Took his daughter and his life . . ." When you know the gentle Vittorio, that sounds a little silly. But still. It's true, of course, that this is the big scene for both of these fathers.

BOOK REVIEW: As powerful absent forces. Mr. Bonati in the form of his ghostly smuggled goods, and

Vittorio's father in the form of the knocking signals that his son, in panic, begins to make.

WOLF HAAS: His father isn't present just in the knocking. The *tock tock tock* noises that he starts sending up, that's exactly like his father. He showed him those when he was a kid, how to make real knocking signals.

BOOK REVIEW: Something about that reminds me of poltergeists.

WOLF HAAS: But even more, his father is present in the accident statistics that immediately start going through his mind.

BOOK REVIEW: It's really awful that he went on and on to the poor kid about all the mining accidents.

WOLF HAAS: You have to be careful before you judge. I think his father just told him in general some heroic stories from the Ruhr. Of course, that was because he himself had the problem that all his ancestors had been miners.

BOOK REVIEW: And he was the first one who wasn't.

WOLF HAAS: He owned this tavern. There was a word that really fascinated me at the beginning, and now it feels perfectly normal. They call every little bar a "tavern."

BOOK REVIEW: He met his young wife at the tavern too.

WOLF HAAS: But not as a customer. Back then she

was his first employee. And he was the first tavern owner in this line of mountaineers. So, subjectively you can understand that he developed this sentimental attachment to the old stories about buddies in the mines. And there was another reason, and I didn't want to include it in the book. It would have gotten too complicated.

BOOK REVIEW: The moment of catastrophe is always the big one for sentimental storytellers.

WOLF HAAS: Right. But I don't think that the father was utterly focused on disasters. You have to say, justifiably, that disasters were all that interested his son. Kids like bloodcurdling stories. At least it's more interesting than most folklore. What the miners called their lockers or their protective clothing — all that local lore about shuttle cars, slickensides, white damp, roof jacks, and all that mining region kielbasa.

BOOK REVIEW: What's kielbasa?

WOLF HAAS: Baloney.

BOOK REVIEW: The body counts and horrifying statistics that raced through his mind when –

WOLF HAAS: Now I'm almost waiting for you to say that you couldn't take it.

BOOK REVIEW: No, actually. It was somehow fascinating. The whole bit about Grimberg and Dahl-busch and so on, just the names you list over and over. The Mother-of-God Shaft.

WOLF HAAS: All the scary facts he'd heard about from

childhood shot through his mind. Alsdorf, 290 dead. Weddinghofen, 405 dead. Luisenthal, 299 dead. Those were all mine explosions.

BOOK REVIEW: Fire in the hole.

WOLF HAAS: Hellfire, exactly. Or the 300 dead in the God's Grace and New Hope Shaft.

BOOK REVIEW: Oh, God's Grace, not Mother-of-God, I'm so stupid. And of course there's always Dahlbusch and Lengede.

WOLF HAAS: Of course always Dahlbusch and Lengede because of the rescued pit men. That was the hope he clung to. In truth, his situation was completely hopeless! It doesn't come across in the book how hopeless it was, thanks to the first person narration. Because of the kiss at the beginning of the book. As a reader, you know he's going to get out of it somehow.

BOOK REVIEW: But as the reader you're even more susceptible to bad surprises than the hero. Here, for example, you still don't know that the kiss Kowalski describes in the beginning, the one on his cheekbone –

WOLF HAAS: One centimeter below his cheekbone –

BOOK REVIEW: – is the one Anni gives him in the intensive care unit.

WOLF HAAS: But the intensive care unit is sure better than being buried alive.

BOOK REVIEW: At least your chances are better.

WOLF HAAS: And you pick up a few kisses.

BOOK REVIEW: He still must have had some hope when he was down there, because he kept sending up the knocking signals. That was hard to deal with when I was reading. This constant *tock tock tock.*

WOLF HAAS: It was hard for him to deal with the fact that he didn't get any answer.

BOOK REVIEW: He soon figured that nobody was looking for him.

WOLF HAAS: And this became more certain the longer nobody came to help him. After half a day he finally knew that there was nothing to see from the outside.

BOOK REVIEW: Or else the mountain rescue team would have been there long ago.

WOLF HAAS: Nobody heard him knocking. The smuggler's den isn't right on the hiking trail; it's at least twenty meters off to the side. Where the cliffs begin. It was completely hopeless that someone might happen to hear him. That's why all the thoughts of all the accident statistics from his childhood went through his mind like shocks in the first few minutes. 103 dead in Maybach. 290 dead in Alsdorf. 51 dead in Stolzenbach. 299 dead in the shaft at Grimberg in Luisenthal. 360 dead in Hamm. 144 dead in Merthyr Tydfil, 114 of them children.

BOOK REVIEW: Stop it!

WOLF HAAS: Yes, the Aberfan Disaster. That's near Swansea where I lived.

BOOK REVIEW: You're almost as obsessed with it as your protagonist Kowalski!

WOLF HAAS: It really is interesting, how that kind of stuff haunts you in a crisis.

BOOK REVIEW: Which reminds me, I think it's particularly interesting that you say "accident statistics of his childhood." There's a lot to that, I think. Maybe he needed the weather statistics later in life as an antidote, to suppress the accident statistics of his childhood.

WOLF HAAS: I'm really thankful that you see him as a statistician in matters of weather. The critics always write that he's an enthusiastic hobby meteorologist and so on. But to me he's more of a statistician than a meteorologist.

BOOK REVIEW: He kept knocking despite the staggering death statistics.

WOLF HAAS: More tirelessly he kept making his *tock tock tocks.* His meager hope had clung to those legendary miraculous mountain rescues. Dalbusch, where they pulled three survivors up 850 meters. And that was in 1955. Without today's technology. Seventy men died in Dahlbusch, but they got three of them out. From 850 meters!

BOOK REVIEW: And especially Lengede, where it took fourteen days to rescue eleven men.

WOLF HAAS: By the way, that's when the rescue capsules that were developed for Dahlbusch were first used. The Dahlbusch Bomb. In Lengede the problem was that at first nobody heard the knocking signs made by the trapped miners. They didn't hear them for fourteen days! That was in 1963. October of '63. There are even TV-documentaries showing the men staggering out of the Dahlbusch Bomb like ghosts, with pitch black faces and, absurdly enough, wearing these really cool sunglasses so they wouldn't be blinded by the light after so many days in the dark.

BOOK REVIEW: And there we've got ghosts again.

WOLF HAAS: What do you mean, "again"?

BOOK REVIEW: As I said before, the *tock tock tock* suggests poltergeists.

WOLF HAAS: But for him those were good ghosts, of course. Because he was clinging to this hope. If other pit men heard the knocking in Lengede after fourteen days, maybe some hiker would hear him.

BOOK REVIEW: I found it especially perverse that the weather frustrated his rescue.

WOLF HAAS: Right. At least it could have been good hiking weather, but it just kept raining. It was hard to take, that Anni's self-indulgent hope for beautiful wedding weather was suddenly a question of life or death for him!

BOOK REVIEW: I wondered how long a person can survive in a situation like that. Without food or fluids.

WOLF HAAS: Basically, it was just incredibly bad luck. Given all the stuff that was there – knitting machines, record players, car tires – Anni's father could at least have stored a carton of canned goods or a case of soda or something. But there was absolutely nothing.

BOOK REVIEW: I thought that when I was reading. And without anything, I'm sure you can't –

WOLF HAAS: Well, without anything a halfway healthy person could survive ten days or so in that situation. The men in Lengede survived for fourteen days, but they had their daily rations with them. And water too.

BOOK REVIEW: Ten days without water?

WOLF HAAS: He managed to find a little water because in a couple of places there were wet spots on the cliff walls.

BOOK REVIEW: So it wasn't just the knocking signs that showed he hadn't given up hope, but even more so the fact that he started his countdown again. 76 hours until the wedding, 70 hours until the wedding, 65 hours until the wedding.

WOLF HAAS: Yes, he doesn't start it right away. Instead –

BOOK REVIEW: By the way, I find it really interesting here that he's counting down to Anni's wedding, of all things. That even in this life-threatening situation, the wedding is still the critical date for him.

WOLF HAAS: Not "still." Before he was buried, he'd already accepted that Anni was going to marry Lukki. At the latest, when she showed him the wedding dress, he was clean.

BOOK REVIEW: Then why does he concentrate his survival countdown on Anni's wedding? And not, for example, on fourteen days, like the rescue of the miners in Lengede – or some other, fictional, rescue date? It almost seems as if his survival were somehow still connected to Anni.

WOLF HAAS: But starting from the moment when he discovers the letters. He didn't uncover them until two days into his ordeal. They were hidden in a crate with a truck battery on top of them as a paperweight. Do you know how heavy a battery with twelve cell plates is?

BOOK REVIEW: No, I've never been a gas station attendant. It's clear to me though, that the letters contain the crucial information, but –

WOLF HAAS: – but we won't talk about that any more today. As a rule, pornographic topics should only be discussed in the morning. An old Farmer's Almanac rule.

Day Five

BOOK REVIEW: Mr. Haas, why do you place so much emphasis on the fact that Vittorio Kowalski missed the important clue in his mother's letter at first?

WOLF HAAS: Now you've fallen into the old journalist's trap and answered your own question.

BOOK REVIEW: Answered what question?

WOLF HAAS: Your question from yesterday. Why he was counting down to the wedding day. Because for him the letters contained two simultaneously critical clues. Before the reference to the crates of weapons really penetrated his brain, he first had to digest the realization that he had been carrying around guilt feelings all these years for absolutely no reason.

BOOK REVIEW: Because at the time, the smuggler wasn't on his way up to his hideout to rescue the two children from the storm.

WOLF HAAS: But to screw his lover.

BOOK REVIEW: Absolutely. And to top it all off, his lover was Vittorio's mother.

WOLF HAAS: Her weakness for Italian family names was stronger than she was.

BOOK REVIEW: Are you trying to bring in something Foucaultesque here? The talk about sex conceals the crucial clue to the crates of weapons?

WOLF HAAS: Did I really make it that obvious that he

didn't find the crates of weapons immediately?

BOOK REVIEW: It only became apparent to me through his blatant justification. Otherwise I would have found it quite normal that this kind of plan doesn't crystallize within seconds.

WOLF HAAS: It's possible that I was justifying something there when nothing needed to be justified. I'm afraid you caught me with an ulterior motive. I was actually just incredibly happy that he didn't start looking for the weapons crates right away. I probably emphasized it because he dithered for two hours. Because otherwise I would have arrived too late.

BOOK REVIEW: But you got to the wedding on time?

WOLF HAAS: I would have gotten there easily anyway if I hadn't gotten lost twice in the last leg of the trip. I had no problem from Gelsenkirchen to the border, no traffic jams at all. Then I went around in a circle. I have a rotten sense of direction.

BOOK REVIEW: We have that in common.

WOLF HAAS: I think it's because I went to boarding school. When you only have to find your way around three sports fields for eight years you don't develop a sense of direction. It's the same with compass points.

BOOK REVIEW: No, I don't think so. It has more to do with the sides of the brain.

WOLF HAAS: In any case I finally found my way there, but when I got to the hotel it was completely empty. Not locked up or anything, but there wasn't a soul around.

BOOK REVIEW: You knew the hotel where Kowalski had booked a room?

WOLF HAAS: From Claudia the secretary. She'd called and reserved the room for him. But it wasn't just the hotel that was empty. The whole village was dead because the wedding ceremony had just started in the church.

BOOK REVIEW: How did you find that out if there wasn't anybody around?

WOLF HAAS: Luckily Mrs. Bachl was sitting on her red bench. She doesn't walk very well any more, at least that's what she says. I suspect, though, that she just doesn't like going to church.

BOOK REVIEW: Probably because she's been sitting on that bench of hers since before churches were invented.

WOLF HAAS: That's what I think.

BOOK REVIEW: But in the book you wrote that Mrs. Bachl sits in the front pew.

WOLF HAAS: Yes, I wanted to have her there in the book, but in reality it was my good luck that I found out everything from her.

BOOK REVIEW: And you got to the church on time?

WOLF HAAS: I wasn't more than five minutes late. I almost didn't make it because the church was completely packed. But it was a good moment to squeeze in because they'd just sung the first hymn, so I didn't miss anything important.

BOOK REVIEW: At that moment Vittorio wasn't quite finished with his explosives yet.

WOLF HAAS: For him, of course, it was a race against time. Now that he knew everything, he definitely wanted to get out before the wedding.

BOOK REVIEW: But he didn't figure it out until two hours before the wedding.

WOLF HAAS: Right, two hours and twelve minutes before the wedding was when he started. He tore up the floor and searched for the weapon crates.

BOOK REVIEW: At that point you were still on the highway.

WOLF HAAS: No, I could have practically been in Farmach if I hadn't driven thirty kilometers in the wrong direction.

BOOK REVIEW: It was really lucky for you that Vittorio didn't begin building the bomb right away.

WOLF HAAS: You're right, it's typical that the idea didn't come to him right away. I didn't have to justify that too much. Anyway, you have to be a real daredevil to blast your way out of a buried bunker.

BOOK REVIEW: It didn't bother me so much that he justifies that. It was more the way he justified why he first overlooks the evidence. Do you think it's really so shocking to discover the sexual escapades of your own parents?

WOLF HAAS: Me?

BOOK REVIEW: We don't want to make the mistake of equating the views of the author with those of the protagonist. But maybe this whole silver star theme comes across as kind of uptight, because you always have the feeling that it's about something else for you, something you don't want to say.

WOLF HAAS: Here it really is about something else, and that's stated clearly. Namely that the guilt feelings that tore Vittorio and Anni apart really stemmed from their parents' secrets.

BOOK REVIEW: That would have precipitated the relapse.

WOLF HAAS: What do you mean by relapse?

BOOK REVIEW: Because you said before that Vittorio had been clean since Anni showed him the wedding dress.

WOLF HAAS: Exactly, that was naturally the mega-relapse. As always with relapses, the latest was worse than before. Now it wasn't just about getting out any more, it was about getting out in time. Before the ceremony!

BOOK REVIEW: And he only had two hours left.

WOLF HAAS: He wanted to do whatever it took to prevent Anni from marrying the wrong man. Under false pretenses. He had to tell her before the wedding what he had discovered in the letters.

BOOK REVIEW: But Anni has known all along that back then her father hadn't gone up to save her. That for all those years her father had been having an affair with Mrs. Kowalski. It was just news to Vittorio. Anni's mother wasn't as discreet as his mother.

WOLF HAAS: Anni knew it already! But Vittorio didn't know that. He believed that Anni was just as clueless as he was. He thought that she would never have married Lukki otherwise.

BOOK REVIEW: A kind of self-imposed penance.

WOLF HAAS: Maybe. In any case, he hoped that –

BOOK REVIEW: – that Anni would reconsider.

WOLF HAAS: Yes, if she found out that all that guilt had been for nothing.

BOOK REVIEW: It has to be said that the guilt feelings had more than just a negative side. You write: "As he ripped out the rotten wood floor under the moldy mattresses, the thought came to him that maybe he had only fallen in love with Anni because his first kiss had cost her father his life."

WOLF HAAS: Yes, that means something to a man.

BOOK REVIEW: If his first kiss offs a girl's father?

WOLF HAAS: You can just chalk that up to puberty, as far as I'm concerned. You can't forget that we're talking about a fifteen-year-old who's going through puberty.

BOOK REVIEW: Very true. But you don't necessarily have to deal with puberty in a pubescent way. And with that I don't mean to say that you do. There's a lot that could be said about this, but now I have to –

WOLF HAAS: Oh! An attack, and no time to defend myself!

BOOK REVIEW: You're the only one who thinks it's boring when other people speak their piece.

WOLF HAAS: Interesting.

BOOK REVIEW: Let's get to the fact that his mother never told him the truth. Although she watched her son develop a little oddly after the incident.

WOLF HAAS: That was pretty crazy. She died just two years before his television appearance –

BOOK REVIEW: His father had died earlier?

WOLF HAAS: Yes, he died a few months after his sixtieth birthday. That's not old, but he lived to be twice as old as his own father.

BOOK REVIEW: Why did he die so young?

WOLF HAAS: I left that out of the book on purpose, because it would have been a digression. Vittorio's grandfather was one of the 70 dead in Dahlbusch.

BOOK REVIEW: So that's why Vittorio's father wasn't allowed to be a miner. Now I get it.

WOLF HAAS: Yes, that topic is a little bit unresolved, I admit. But nonetheless I decided to leave it out. Otherwise the reader would also be buried with too many references, so to speak.

BOOK REVIEW: But it's a shame that you left it out of the book! One would have had a better understanding of why he's so sentimental about mines.

WOLF HAAS: In any case, Vittorio's father had already been dead for a few years. So it really wouldn't have been a problem for his mother to tell her secret. Just say to her grown son, listen, all that guilt –

BOOK REVIEW: – you can forget about it.

WOLF HAAS: Exactly. At some point, as an old lady you can admit that you once lived. Say that you had a passionate summer romance with the landlord for years while you were on vacation. And really exaggerated your asthma so there could be no alternative to the yearly trips to that place with the "fresh air."

BOOK REVIEW: I got the impression that her son suspected her of faking the asthma.

WOLF HAAS: A highly stylized shortage of breath! But you can admit that too, when you're old and explain to your son that his kiddie stuff wasn't the only drama on that stormy day.

BOOK REVIEW: The kids' mistake was seeking shelter in their parents' love nest.

WOLF HAAS: And they didn't penetrate as far in as the real love nest. They were on the upper level, on the ground floor hayloft. And underneath, where Vittorio was now trapped, where his mother used to meet Bonati – that was where the real love nest was. Everything was there; the whole floor was outfitted with mattresses, which was really lucky for him when he fell through the stairs. The smuggler's den was more camouflage for the love nest than anything else.

BOOK REVIEW: Actually, a double camouflage. On top, the hay was a cover for the smuggler's den in the cellar. But down below the smuggled goods were, mostly, a cover for the love nest.

WOLF HAAS: And of course they each took separate ways up the mountain. He usually drove up the timber road with his motorcycle, which was the way he used to deliver the goods with his jeep as well. She just walked up the hiking path. That's why Mrs. Kowalski could still turn back when it suddenly got dark. She came home looking like a drowned rat. As if she'd been dunked.

BOOK REVIEW: Like Vittorio as a child when Lukki pushed him off the air mattress at the swimming pool.

WOLF HAAS: And Anni's father was already up on the mountain when the storm arrived and wanted to take cover in his smuggler's den.

BOOK REVIEW: In the smuggler's den-slash-love-nest. Where his daughter was lying stark naked with her boyfriend in the hay.

WOLF HAAS: And didn't let her father in. Exactly.

BOOK REVIEW: And now, fifteen years later, Vittorio couldn't get out.

WOLF HAAS: (*laughs*) That's love. Either you can't get in or you can't get out.

BOOK REVIEW: Well, okay. You didn't write that in the book. That really sounds more like Riemer.

WOLF HAAS: Now you're back to the silver star orgasm.

BOOK REVIEW: Not without good reason. I take it that's why you gave so much space to Riemer's silver star theory at the beginning of the book, because of Mrs. Kowalski's flowery description in her letter of how she lost consciousness in her lover's arms.

WOLF HAAS: I wanted to make sure it didn't just concern Mrs. Kowalski.

BOOK REVIEW: But unlike Mrs. Kowalski, Riemer never experienced it.

WOLF HAAS: Oh come on! Riemer just read somewhere once that the better the sex, the worse you remember it. So, mediocre sex, good memories; terrific sex, bad memories. Silver star sex, no memory at all.

BOOK REVIEW: Is that actually true?

WOLF HAAS: Whew, don't ask me. At any rate, at first Vittorio was utterly fixated on this part of the letter. For most people it's a strange topic, the sexuality of their parents. You don't have to be as naive as the good Vittorio to not want to know about it. And now he has to read the graphic depiction of how his mother – in complete and absolute –

BOOK REVIEW: – whatever.

WOLF HAAS: No, please, not again. In complete and absolute –

BOOK REVIEW: – complete and absolute ecstasy.

WOLF HAAS: Yes, that's it, beautiful. Ecstasy. How his mother fainted with bliss. In other words, Riemer's highest category, silver star.

BOOK REVIEW: I have to ask you something important about that later. I have a deep suspicion. You probably already know what I mean. And so I don't forget it, I'll put my watch on my right wrist. That irritates me so much that I can't stop thinking about it.

WOLF HAAS: Good trick.

BOOK REVIEW: It's like tying a knot in my handkerchief.

WOLF HAAS: Yeah, people don't do that anymore. But we could talk about it now, that way you don't have to –

BOOK REVIEW: No, let's finish with Vittorio's mother's silver star swoon. She describes her faint in such purple prose that in one place in her fairly baroque fantasy, the crates of weapons, which have been moldering under the floor of this love nest for decades, explode.

WOLF HAAS: That was the crucial information.

BOOK REVIEW: By the way, I think that's a very

poetic passage.

WOLF HAAS: Yes, that's original text from the letter. I toned it down a little. Otherwise it would have been, "Haas, what a pig." Besides, at points it was really hard to deal with the way his mother writes that the weapons crates under them, ignited by their passion, explode and shoot them both high up into the heavens. Of course those are things you don't normally write down. As an artifact, it's just as problematic, it becomes your own text as soon as you include it. But you feel better about it.

BOOK REVIEW: Because you yourself aren't responsible for it.

WOLF HAAS: Yes, probably. One thing less for the censorship board. But I didn't have a choice anyway. I had to put it in the book to make it believable that her son needed some time to grasp it.

BOOK REVIEW: That he was really supposed to be focusing on the weapons crates.

WOLF HAAS: Precious minutes were being wasted! But you're right, maybe I wouldn't have emphasized it so much if I hadn't come to it just at the last moment.

BOOK REVIEW: It wasn't 'til a good two hours before Anni's wedding that he had pulled up enough floor-boards to get to the weapons crates.

WOLF HAAS: Right, he exposed the first crate just two hours and five minutes before the ceremony. Unfortunately it was locked.

BOOK REVIEW: One hour and fifty eight minutes before the wedding he got it open.

WOLF HAAS: But there was nothing inside but machine guns, ancient Mausers from World War II. When he finally got the crate with the hand-grenades open, only one and a half hours were left. And right after that, the landmines. From this point on, he was on auto-pilot.

BOOK REVIEW: I thought that part was a little difficult. As a woman I didn't do military service or anything like that.

WOLF HAAS: Same here. I did alternative service with the Red Cross.

BOOK REVIEW: Oh, that's interesting.

WOLF HAAS: By the way, in Austria you say something like "alternative servant" and in Germany it's "alternative service." I think that says a lot about the difference between the two countries.

BOOK REVIEW: What do you mean, "servant"?

WOLF HAAS: I don't know anything about hand grenades and landmines. But it was less difficult for Kowalski. First, he had done his time with the military. In Recklinghausen. Second, as an engineer, he had a certain fundamental competence.

BOOK REVIEW: I figured. He detached the pin from a hand grenade and attached it to a landmine.

WOLF HAAS: Basically, it wasn't anything more than

that. Except he connected three landmines together to get more explosive power. The principle was simply to remove the top and bottom parts of the landmines and use the pins from the hand grenades as fuses.

BOOK REVIEW: Because they have a delayed fuse, as I understand it.

WOLF HAAS: Yes, otherwise the grenade would explode in the thrower's hand. You know that from war movies, I'm sure. The soldier pulls the pin and throws the grenade and only after five seconds or so does it explode over on enemy territory.

BOOK REVIEW: And for him that was enough time to take cover. I was amazed that someone could survive an explosion like that in the same room and not get blown to pieces by the blast.

WOLF HAAS: That's what I thought, but it doesn't work like that. In cases of planned explosions, for example in blasting for tunnels, the explosives expert is often down inside. Basically, you can do it that way too.

BOOK REVIEW: But presumably the conditions are better.

WOLF HAAS: They sure are! He couldn't be sure he'd survive.

BOOK REVIEW: He knew for certain that after the explosion he'd be buried.

WOLF HAAS: Nothing else was possible! His only hope was the smuggler's den would be so damaged that it would be visible from outside and give somebody the idea to look for him in there. But also that the ledge wouldn't be so completely destroyed that he'd be buried alive. That's also why it was so important to calibrate the charge.

BOOK REVIEW: Too little or too much –

WOLF HAAS: Exactly – shows an idiot's touch. Where did you get that?

BOOK REVIEW: Well, from your book.

WOLF HAAS: Oh, I thought I cut that out.

BOOK REVIEW: Later a lot of people said that it had been a suicide attempt. That Kowalski just wanted to end his suffering down there.

WOLF HAAS: That made him really mad. That was in some local paper. It's a real insult. I think it didn't just hurt him as a human being because nobody likes to be accused of attempted suicide. It also damaged his pride as an engineer.

BOOK REVIEW: There's nothing you can do against rumors like that.

WOLF HAAS: Naturally it was a lucky thing for me. I can barely believe he would have been so open with me if it hadn't been in his interest to set the record straight.

BOOK REVIEW: Although you have to say you also get the feeling as you're reading that he does act with a kind of suicidal purpose.

WOLF HAAS: Yes, it was a hara-kiri action. Forty-seven minutes before Anni's wedding, he removed the detonator from the hand grenade.

BOOK REVIEW: In the book it says "I removed the explosive core like a cook removing the inedible parts of a fruit."

WOLF HAAS: Then he placed this fuse on the open end of the first landmine.

BOOK REVIEW: This comparison with coring a piece of fruit is almost sensual.

WOLF HAAS: Without a certain sensual delight in nuts and bolts, an operation like this is doomed to failure.

BOOK REVIEW: There's something trancelike about it, the way you describe the efficient handling of the highly explosive materials. You write that he was thinking about the weather the entire time.

WOLF HAAS: I believe that gave him the necessary calm and confidence.

BOOK REVIEW: You even write that his thoughts about the tropopause, you know, about the lid that holds the stratosphere on the troposphere, prompted him to attach a fourth landmine. He's obsessed with this phenomenon. He mentions it again and again.

WOLF HAAS: But in this situation he has good reason, because of the way the powerful updrafts create violent storms by lifting the lid and letting the clouds press up into the stratosphere. On the surface he thought about the tropopause, but in reality he was busy getting the calibration right! It's just like writing. You're always thinking about something different from what you're really thinking about at the moment.

BOOK REVIEW: Or like driving a car, when you start daydreaming instead of reading the signs.

WOLF HAAS: Exactly! At this point I would have already been in Farmach if I hadn't missed the signpost because I was dreaming about the best way to address Kowalski. I thought I'd find him in the hotel. And the first contact is particularly important so people don't shut you down right from the start.

BOOK REVIEW: But in the final analysis it didn't matter that you came too late.

WOLF HAAS: It wasn't up to me. It was up to him. For him every second counted. And the precise calibration. He was making life or death decisions while he seemed to be thinking about the weather.

BOOK REVIEW: The charge had to be big enough to lift the debris that covered him.

WOLF HAAS: If the bomb exploded without shifting the debris, he would have been a goner. But at the same time the charge couldn't be so big that he'd be buried kilometers deep and just get crushed.

BOOK REVIEW: And on top of that was the problem that the five-second fuse wouldn't give him enough time to take cover.

WOLF HAAS: That's why – four minutes before the nuptial mass – he starts to unravel the sweater.

BOOK REVIEW: The sweater that Anni had knitted for him fifteen years earlier. The one he wore under his blazer on Gottschalk's show.

WOLF HAAS: He just liked wearing it. It was a light sweater.

BOOK REVIEW: Without which he never felt properly dressed.

WOLF HAAS: And now this tic of his saved his life.

BOOK REVIEW: That drives you half crazy when you read it! In the meantime, the ceremony had begun while he's calmly unraveling the sweater to braid a long fuse from the wool.

WOLF HAAS: If I'd known that, I wouldn't have spent such a long time standing with Mrs. Bachl.

BOOK REVIEW: For him it was a catastrophe that he didn't have the explosives finished before the wedding started.

WOLF HAAS: Thank God he realized it wasn't the beginning that was crucial, but the moment when they exchange vows. It was his good luck that Anni had so thoroughly described the impending wedding ceremony. He knew that he still had nearly a half-hour. Otherwise he would have just said what the hell and risked it without a long fuse. And so he took his time, but he was extremely nervous and kept tangling the yarn.

BOOK REVIEW: It wasn't until twenty minutes before the vows that he started to climb.

WOLF HAAS: Now it all came down to his climbing skills.

BOOK REVIEW: In other words, the thing he rejected in his father.

WOLF HAAS: It always embarrassed him that his father had been Bonati's rival. Only in his situation he had no choice. If he hadn't put the improvised explosive as high up as possible, in the chink in the dirt that faced the exit, there would have been no chance that any of the debris up there would shift in the right direction.

BOOK REVIEW: Here you have another chance to satisfy your counting addiction.

WOLF HAAS: How so? Because fifteen minutes before the vows he hadn't covered even half the climbing distance?

BOOK REVIEW: No, that's not what I mean. I'm talking about your overly detailed explanation of the degree of difficulty of the climb. In the passage where the reader has already died a thousand deaths and still wants to know if he makes it in time or not, you go off on a protracted tangent about his father's climbing career. How he slowly progressed from the first level of difficulty to the second and from the second to the third. He climbs a Level One, he climbs a Level Two, he climbs a Level Three, he climbs a Level Four.

WOLF HAAS: Who?

BOOK REVIEW: Ugh, his father, who had an irrepressible ambition to someday climb an overhang.

WOLF HAAS: (*laughs*) An overhang? In his dreams!

BOOK REVIEW: But his son has just reached an overhang.

WOLF HAAS: From below he thought he could avoid the overhang. He could only get the explosive into the crevice if he climbed up the wall. Well, the wall wasn't so difficult. It wasn't more than a Level Four, maybe a Five in places.

BOOK REVIEW: But at the top he knew he couldn't get close enough. He could only reach that essential crevice if he climbed a few meters out onto the overhang.

WOLF HAAS: I was just fascinated by the unbelievable physical feats that a person is capable of when his life is in danger.

BOOK REVIEW: Well, he wasn't even a trained climber.

WOLF HAAS: Far from it! He had no idea about climbing. As a child he completely refused to do any climbing, to his father's dismay. Otherwise, he wasn't even in training, where you could at least say he was that strong because he worked out every day at the gym. Pull-ups and stuff. Nothing! Riemer was in better shape than he was. He went at least twice a week to that new gym, "Trainsporting," on Bochum Street. But Vittorio Kowalski, he was just about as athletic as I am! So, it's really incredible how he got up that wall.

BOOK REVIEW: He was also trapped in there for days without food. He must have been extremely weak.

WOLF HAAS: Yes, on top of all that. He climbed up the wall in that condition, with the lamp on his head and the explosives on his belt, the way his ancestors carried the emergency oxygen masks.

BOOK REVIEW: That's like something out of *Spider-man*.

WOLF HAAS: A lot of this can be explained by the energy produced by the fear of death. And then the wall, but next, the overhang! That doesn't make sense to me. Seven minutes before the vows he climbs out onto the overhang.

BOOK REVIEW: Six minutes before the vows he remembered the fight between his father and Mr. Bonati about whether strength or technique is more important for climbing an overhang.

WOLF HAAS: That was really more his father's discussion. He liked to theorize about the latest developments, the newest equipment, the newest climbing technique, and Bonati just said condescendingly: "If Lord Schmalz says no, it's no."

BOOK REVIEW: Excuse me?

WOLF HAAS: It doesn't work if you don't know that "Schmalz" means strength.

BOOK REVIEW: Okay, okay. That's what it says in the book. It doesn't work without the Schmalz. But you just said it differently. Lord Schmalz?

WOLF HAAS: Ah. He just said stuff like that sometimes. Mindless poetry, sort of. He was paraphrasing a folk song that goes something like "If the Lord God doesn't want it, there's no help for it." It's kind of a weepy, kitschy Viennese song. And to make fun of his summer guest's weak theory, he turned "Lord God" into "Lord Schmalz."

BOOK REVIEW: And if he doesn't want it, it will not happen. Got it. Biceps as God.

WOLF HAAS: Biceps as God – does sound ridiculous, but it was pretty appropriate for the situation Vittorio was in.

BOOK REVIEW: Except he did it with technology.

WOLF HAAS: We'll never know.

BOOK REVIEW: Basically, what stood behind these fathers' debate was the problem of theory vs. practice.

WOLF HAAS: The technology-schmalz debate. Vittorio recalled the debate earlier, but six minutes before the vows he suddenly got the feeling that they were both helping him. A kind of New Age feeling that his father was helping from the grave with technology and Mr. Bonati was helping with strength.

BOOK REVIEW: Of course that's a pretty conciliatory concept. If Mr. Bonati is helping him, he must have forgiven him. And five minutes before the vows, Vittorio does the crucial pull-up.

WOLF HAAS: I hope it doesn't sound that drastic when you read it. I mean, the crucial pull-up and that sort of thing. Basically, it was just edging a few centimeters forward. Of course, in fact, every centimeter is crucial, so in a sense you can't make one false move or lose your strength.

BOOK REVIEW: What impressed me most was how you described the emotional pressure. It reminded me of the danger of getting the bends when you go deep sea diving.

WOLF HAAS: I don't dive. As a child I got really bad middle ear infections.

BOOK REVIEW: Middle ear, isn't that where your sense of balance comes from?

WOLF HAAS: Everything's fine with my sense of balance. My hearing is also fine, I just shouldn't go diving.

BOOK REVIEW: Anyway, you write that the greatest danger in climbing an overhang is not that you lose your strength, but … wait, here it is: "The dangerous thing about climbing an overhang is not that the strength leaves your fingers. The most dangerous thing is not the lame arms, shaking knees, unbearable calf cramps, or numb toes. The dangerous thing about an overhang is that you start to confuse up and down." Is that really true?

WOLF HAAS: For a moment you're consumed by the deceptive feeling of weightlessness. And like a driver who lets go of the wheel for a minute in the fast lane at two hundred kilometers per hour, the climber on the overhang feels the temptation to let go of the cliff for a second.

BOOK REVIEW: The way you describe that, the

overcoming of gravity, it's like levitation.

WOLF HAAS: Like what?

BOOK REVIEW: Like the levitations of the great mystics.

WOLF HAAS: No. Yes. Well, what should I say? That sounds too flamboyant for me. You and your mystics! But let's just leave it at that. I needed a little of that feeling to lift him out of that – so to speak, out of the world of gravity. But that wasn't because I wanted to make climbing overhangs into something mystical, rather I had to change the narrative perspective.

BOOK REVIEW: Because suddenly you're down at the wedding.

WOLF HAAS: No, not suddenly, but, but, but –

BOOK REVIEW: – seamlessly.

WOLF HAAS: Yes, that was a big problem for me. The whole book was told from his subjective viewpoint, but I definitely wanted to see the explosion from outside.

BOOK REVIEW: You wanted to describe it from your perspective.

WOLF HAAS: Once I'd finally found it! But a one-time change of perspective is a literary trick. That's not permitted.

BOOK REVIEW: That's like when Hemingway describes how the lion feels when it's shot.

WOLF HAAS: That's why I let him climb over things a little bit, so with each pull-up he kind of climbs out of his own reality and hoists himself into the festive light of the wedding ceremony.

BOOK REVIEW: And he counts down the minutes again. The effect is sort of like a mantra.

WOLF HAAS: All the previous countdowns, the way he approaches the border crossing, the way the storm advances and skips any linear development, I needed all of that just to set up this counting. Actually, one writes an entire book to prepare one single incredible passage that the reader will swallow, so to speak.

BOOK REVIEW: You use this formula a lot, that the reader should swallow a passage. Somehow that doesn't sound very friendly.

WOLF HAAS: The way he climbs onto the overhang is in and of itself almost impossible to tell in a believable way.

BOOK REVIEW: Well, I swallowed it.

WOLF HAAS: And then that the story comes out down in the village at the wedding, that wouldn't have been possible without the counting. But that's how I could sort of slowly make it come alive: seven minutes to the vows, as the priest says this and that to the congregation, six minutes to the vows, as the congregation gets up after kneeling, five more minutes to the vows, as Anni –

BOOK REVIEW: At first you still believe he's just imagining this.

WOLF HAAS: Exactly. But sentence by sentence I, as the narrator, was able to get him down to the brightly lighted church, while in real time he was actually still scrabbling around in the darkness.

BOOK REVIEW: The decisive point is that here your narrator's perspective for the first time is identical with your personal perspective.

WOLF HAAS: For me it was simply the problem of how I was to get outside fictionally while the first person narrator is still locked inside. How does the narrative uncouple from the narrator, so to speak? What kind of drugs do I have to give him to detach him – the way a bit of sound in a film can signal a flash-forward?

BOOK REVIEW: You could have made it easy on yourself and told the whole thing with film-editing technique, alternating between his and Anni's perspectives.

WOLF HAAS: Yes, true, I could have made it easy on myself and just not written the book at all!

BOOK REVIEW: The ease you don't permit yourself, you give your hero, in spades. You explain that with a kind of paradoxical attraction to the earth. "The closer I got to the ground above me, the stronger was its attraction. Centimeter by centimeter I climbed into a weightless state and – "

WOLF HAAS: In fact, of course, his fingers were bleeding. That much is clear, but I couldn't write that because the story was supposed to move to the church and I wanted to prevent it from turning into a martyrdom. That's why I depicted the climbing as more weightless than it actually was. And I completely left out the severed toe.

BOOK REVIEW: Oh, no. That must have been hard for you.

WOLF HAAS: Yes, this is my first book where nobody loses a body part.

BOOK REVIEW: Well, in the book you depict that in a completely different way! "I pulled myself up as if gravity were lifting me upward, as the priest told the bridal couple to rise. I heard the mother of the bride sobbing, I heard the organ playing, I heard Mrs. Bachl crying, I heard the congregation coughing, I heard the priest asking the congregation to follow the bride and groom and rise for the wedding vows. And I heard the creaking kneeling-benches groan under the weight of the bodies raising themselves with their last strength. I'd been crouching motionless for so long in the pew that I couldn't feel my knees anymore, but I managed to pull myself up two centimeters at the priest's behest."

WOLF HAAS: Yeah, phew. Finally I was in the story down at the church.

BOOK REVIEW: Three minutes before the vows, while your hero was still up there clinging to the overhang like a bat.

WOLF HAAS: Nowhere did I write "like a bat."

BOOK REVIEW: The image just came to me, also because you call attention to the beautiful candlelight in the church as Kowalski sits trapped up there in the darkness.

WOLF HAAS: But not for much longer.

BOOK REVIEW: Here your story comes apart for a moment not only spatially, but temporally, when you reveal that three days later there will be a coffin in the place where the bride and groom are now standing.

WOLF HAAS: Yes, true, but that's a normal foreshadowing. Just the way Kowalski sometimes does it. In that sense it's not a change in perspective. He just says that the deceased for whom the same church bells are supposed to ring three days later wasn't –

BOOK REVIEW: – and for whom the same people will again dress in their Sunday best –

WOLF HAAS: Exactly – and whose flower-covered casket will stand in the same place in front of the altar –

BOOK REVIEW: – in the same place where the bride and groom rose for the exchange of wedding rings that everyone was waiting for –

WOLF HAAS: – he was not the deceased.

BOOK REVIEW: He says: "The deceased, to whom three days later the same village priest – who was now calling on Anni and Lukki to raise themselves up and seal their union with a kiss – would bid farewell forever, that deceased wasn't me."

WOLF HAAS: That's all he says.

BOOK REVIEW: When you read this passage, it's almost maddening how you describe the wedding guests in such a detailed way. Here, of all places, when all you want to know is if, and how, Vittorio Kowalski escapes, you lose yourself in the artistry of describing Anni's wedding dress. When it first appeared three days ago, Anni called the color "vanilla."

WOLF HAAS: Three days and seven hours ago, yes.

BOOK REVIEW: And now it says it was by no means vanilla. And then there follow some digressions about vanilla ice cream at the swimming pool and you even give the price of a scoop of vanilla ice cream at that time.

WOLF HAAS: Yes, one scoop, one shilling. A long time ago. Personally, I can still remember when it was fifty groschen. You're not allowed to write that though because it makes me look old.

BOOK REVIEW: And the narrator who finds himself in extreme danger also narrows the definition, by saying that "vanilla" doesn't mean the artificial color of vanilla ice cream. Well, in the candle light the dress wasn't the color of real vanilla either.

WOLF HAAS: My mother always said to me that when you're buying a piece of clothing you should always go to the door and look at it in natural light because artificial light can play tricks.

BOOK REVIEW: Oh, that was your mother? In the book you have Vittorio's mother say that.

WOLF HAAS: It doesn't matter, all the mothers of the world have said that. Always go to the door! To the daylight! Don't judge by artificial light!

BOOK REVIEW: While Anni's wedding dress glows in the most wondrous mood lighting, in the darkness of the smuggler's den, Vittorio's headlamp grows dimmer as he pushes himself forward millimeter by millimeter.

WOLF HAAS: The beautiful light that pours through the colorful stained glass windows is also the first indication that the sun came out during the mass.

BOOK REVIEW: But you don't understand that yet in this passage. You're so solidly in the church that you're not thinking about the weather outside.

WOLF HAAS: No, you're only supposed to get it later. Here it's just a kind of preparation. Primarily I wanted to savor it because it was really an unbelievably beautiful light.

BOOK REVIEW: You write that Vittorio's mother, or your mother, always said that in clothing stores they had a special light that made everything look good. And then it says further on, "They must have that kind of light in churches too."

WOLF HAAS: It was like in a Tarkovski film or something, the thousand candle flames, and Anni's dress reflected the candlelight and the golden baroque altar and the colorful stained glass windows and the sea of flowers in which the bride seemed to swim. I couldn't even bring myself to write it.

BOOK REVIEW: You're hooked.

WOLF HAAS: How do you mean that?

BOOK REVIEW: This woman. You would have liked her too.

WOLF HAAS: I can't describe a bride without getting hooked on her as I write. I've also described murderers.

BOOK REVIEW: You write, "the bride was surrounded by such a glow that it was barely possible for me to refrain from taking my aching hands off the back of the stone pew in front of me just for a second to applaud in appreciation."

WOLF HAAS: The bit with the hands isn't exactly my perspective! That's the last remnant of the "I," if you will, still seen from Kowalski's point of view, which still clings from the overhang. That's the joke here. If he claps his hands impulsively, he's dead.

BOOK REVIEW: Because in reality he isn't gripping the church pew, but the overhang.

WOLF HAAS: Thus, the aching hands.

BOOK REVIEW: And the "stone" pew. That's clear. This cross-fade technique, where the last shadows of Kowalski's actual situation sort of shine through. However. The view of Anni and her groom is from the last pew. Is that where you sat?

WOLF HAAS: No. I stood in back where the people stand who aren't really listening. Sort of in the church doorway. In the vestibule, I don't know what you call that.

BOOK REVIEW: You not only describe the mood lighting in the church in great detail, but also Anni's bridal coiffure. It says that, from the pews, it seemed as if the bride and the groom were almost the same height as they stood before the priest.

WOLF HAAS: Yes, and when they were kneeling Anni was even taller than him! Because of her wedding updo. Her hair made her about a head taller. And there were some white flowers artfully arranged in her dark hair, white orange blossoms, but from far away they almost looked like tiny flames or fireflies lighting her head.

BOOK REVIEW: Did it infuriate you that one critic somewhat gloatingly found this mistake – the chapter where Anni shows him the dress talks about a hat that hasn't been delivered yet, but now she's clearly not wearing a hat because she has her hair up?

WOLF HAAS: No. It's true, that's a mistake. That kind of thing always happens to me somewhere.

BOOK REVIEW: When I was reading it, I thought she'd changed her mind.

WOLF HAAS: No, it was my mistake. I wrote that the hat was being delivered because I didn't want to write what she really said, which was that the garter hadn't been delivered.

BOOK REVIEW: The bashful author.

WOLF HAAS: And so I overlooked the fact that a hat wouldn't go with her hairdo.

BOOK REVIEW: Yes, it would have been a shame to cover that hairdo with a hat. It sounds magical the way you write, "The orange blossoms flickered in her hair."

WOLF HAAS: Yes, and her neck was so delicate that you had to ask yourself how it could carry the weight of the bouffant hairdo and the flowers at all.

BOOK REVIEW: I must say, I found the way you describe her delicate neck a bit over the top.

WOLF HAAS: But the reason you found it exaggerated was that I understated it. Anni's neck is actually really – well, I had to scale it down somehow, so I cut and cut so it wouldn't come across as overdone. But when you scale it back too far, it sometimes has the effect of being poorly conceived.

BOOK REVIEW: An old farmer's almanac rule.

WOLF HAAS: Exactly. And it wasn't just her neck. Her long, billowing dress sank into the sea of flowers in such a way that you couldn't think of anything but a swan the lemon color of a brimstone butterfly.

BOOK REVIEW: Okay, I understand that you at least left out the brimstone butterfly. That really would have been over the top.

WOLF HAAS: It wouldn't have amazed me if, while the priest was flipping and flipping through his thick book, this swan had elegantly and gracefully swum away. Glided away, I should say. You never see swans really swimming; they glide so elegantly over the surface of the water.

BOOK REVIEW: Like air mattresses.

WOLF HAAS: More like sailboats. Like sailboats in the

night. Or like brides in a sea of flowers.

BOOK REVIEW: Whatever. In any case, Anni didn't glide away over the sea of flowers in the church. she listened devoutly to the words the priest had begun to read out of his big golden book.

WOLF HAAS: The priest read: "If anyone here has just cause why they should not lawfully be joined in marriage, speak now, or forever hold your peace."

BOOK REVIEW: Correct me if I'm wrong, but that doesn't actually belong to the Catholic wedding rite in our area. It comes from American films or something.

WOLF HAAS: Exactly. And he didn't read it out of his golden book either, he'd stuck it in on a Post-it note.

BOOK REVIEW: Oh that's why he was constantly leafing through his thick book. He was searching for the butterfly-colored Post-it.

WOLF HAAS: Exactly. The heavy book had sort of absorbed the Post-it. It took him forever to find it.

BOOK REVIEW: A small culture clash.

WOLF HAAS: Anni just knew it – like us – from thousands of American films. She badgered the priest so he would say it at her wedding.

BOOK REVIEW: Lucky for Vittorio. Otherwise he would have been much too late.

WOLF HAAS: That was lucky for him. I'm not New Age or anything. Telepathy and that kind of stuff, I can't stand it, but that the priest spent so long thumbing through pages in the book, and after that, he still hesitated for such a long time –

BOOK REVIEW: You're the third person this month who's said "I'm not New Age or anything, but…"

WOLF HAAS: Yes, well. That's what it's like with strange coincidences. People like it when there's something meaningful or emblematic tied to it.

BOOK REVIEW: You devote many pages to the priest's long hesitation.

WOLF HAAS: It really was unbearable. Even I got nervous. It was probably just the usual priestly slowness.

BOOK REVIEW: It almost reads as if he wanted to use his hesitation to encourage someone to object to the wedding.

WOLF HAAS: Maybe he just didn't know how to proceed because it was an unfamiliar passage.

BOOK REVIEW: In your novel, though, you get the feeling that he senses something. Or maybe he knows from someone's confession that Anni is marrying the wrong man. He asks his question and then looks around for much too long.

WOLF HAAS: Yes, his gaze seemed to scan the room as if he were trying to see into the soul of each individual wedding guest.

BOOK REVIEW: I don't know if I'm allowed to ask you. If it's too personal we'll just leave it out.

WOLF HAAS: Shoot.

BOOK REVIEW: The second time I read it, I had the suspicion that you left the church at exactly this point.

WOLF HAAS: Me?

BOOK REVIEW: No?

WOLF HAAS: Yes. But that wasn't because of the priest's question. I had no objection to the union of Anni and Lukki.

BOOK REVIEW: Besides the fact that men always have something against an attractive woman marrying another man.

WOLF HAAS: At the back where I was standing people were constantly going in and out, the smokers, the talkers, etc. And the uneasy mood in the church was just too much for me, the way the priest said "Speak now or forever hold your peace," and then just stopped. I found that unbearable! He just kept looking around, and I'm sure I wasn't the only one who felt nervous.

BOOK REVIEW: Yes.

WOLF HAAS: But how did you figure out that I left?

BOOK REVIEW: It wasn't hard. You describe the scene like this. "'Speak now, or forever hold your peace,' said the priest in a voice so loud that it boomed through the whole church and even out into the churchyard." Then the narrative moves outdoors for the first time.

WOLF HAAS: True. If I expected such close readers I could never write another word again.

BOOK REVIEW: No, it really wasn't hard to figure out. You describe it down to the last detail. What was inside the church door. The two saints' statues to the left and right of the entrance, and hidden behind them, loudspeakers that broadcast the ceremonies outside so the overflow crowd hears the question that the priest asks over and over in your novel.

WOLF HAAS: But it was clear that he only asked the question once.

BOOK REVIEW: He asked the question only once, but the text keeps circling around that single question again and again.

WOLF HAAS: Strange, in the book I always wrote the priest's "question," and now that you mention it, it occurs to me that it isn't a question at all: "Speak now, or forever hold your peace" is, strictly speaking, not a question but –

BOOK REVIEW: – a command.

WOLF HAAS: Yes, a sort of combined request and appeal. Actually it's more a demand for silence. If you don't say anything now, you should keep your trap shut in the future. Nonetheless, people take it as a question somehow: by any chance is there anybody who has some objection? At least that's how I took it in this situation, so it's really an awkward question. Almost like in *Crimewatch* where you get the feeling that they're asking you if there's a fugitive mass murderer hiding somewhere among your friends and family.

BOOK REVIEW: *Crimewatch* does it for you?

WOLF HAAS: I thought of it because it's so hardboiled. *Crimewatch* is always so tough and has a serious sort of tone.

BOOK REVIEW: Inquisitional.

WOLF HAAS: And the priest's voice took on an intimidating tone. The effect was even stronger outdoors. You mustn't forget that in this Alpine region the churches stand in the middle of cemeteries, or the cemeteries surround the church, depending on how you look at it. Anyway, the people outside in the cemetery almost always have the best seats at weddings. Even after the ceremony, when the couple comes out – for throwing rice, etc.

BOOK REVIEW: Like the die-hards who buy standing-room tickets at the opera.

WOLF HAAS: The people inside are almost marginalized. At the front of the pack but really a little bit out of the picture. The communication is taking place outside in the cemetery. And the priest can be heard just as well through the speakers as from inside. At worst, the voice that came from behind the stone statues to the left and the right of the entrance sounded a little hollow: *If anyone here has just cause why Anni and Lukki should not lawfully be joined in marriage, speak now, or forever hold your peace.*

BOOK REVIEW: And everyone kept silent, of course.

WOLF HAAS: They all kept silent. The only sound was the sobbing from the first pews. Anni's mother, the only one of the four parents still alive, and the aunts and cousins all cried a little to themselves. And because they were sitting so far up front, the microphones broadcast it all outside.

BOOK REVIEW: There's always a lot of crying at weddings. Sometimes I think more than at funerals.

WOLF HAAS: And the reasons aren't really clear. Probably they're mixed, which is why people say they're "stirred up."

BOOK REVIEW: Pun-free zone. In the book, though, you write, "Maybe a few of the tears were shed because Anni was about to marry the wrong man."

WOLF HAAS: Yes, but I think that's more wishful thinking on the part of the author, that the quiz show champion Kowalski would have secret sympathizers. The truth is closer to your laconic observation that there's always a lot of crying at weddings.

BOOK REVIEW: And one always marries the wrong man.

WOLF HAAS: (*laughs*) You said it, not me.

BOOK REVIEW: What would have interested me the most here, though, are Anni's own thoughts about her decision at this moment. She told Vittorio on his first day at the Hotel Schwalbenwandblick that she cried herself to sleep after she saw him on television, but after that night she seems to have made up her mind. As witness, her little fashion show with the wedding dress.

WOLF HAAS: "Fashion show," that's good. The

question is still open, though, what or who is being shown: the dress, or Vittorio.

BOOK REVIEW: We've had that discussion, but how Anni really feels at the wedding is not quite clear. You write that you couldn't tell if the bride was crying.

WOLF HAAS: She could only be seen from behind. Actually, I left the church at that point. When her shoulders began to shake, I was out of there.

BOOK REVIEW: You can't stand to see a woman cry.

WOLF HAAS: Ha ha. I admit there's a certain romance to it, the wish that, when someone marries for love, they weep. And that the bride isn't thinking, "So what? He's the wrong guy anyway," the way you just put it so well. "And the main thing is, he's got a hotel, etc."

BOOK REVIEW: That's too unromantic for you.

WOLF HAAS: Well, it's hard to write a love story if you don't give the characters a little romance.

BOOK REVIEW: Women have to cry to make it romantic?

WOLF HAAS: To this day I'm still not sure if Anni cried at all.

BOOK REVIEW: You write that other than the sobbing from the first pews you couldn't hear anything while the priest let his silence just hang over the heads of the congregation for what seemed like an eternity.

WOLF HAAS: Yes, well. Outside you could hear all

kinds of things. Cars driving by in the distance, bicycle bells, birds, etc., but for me it wasn't about a realistic soundscape or anything like that. Right away it gets too impressionistic if you mention dogs barking or the drone of airplanes. For me this passage was simply about the silence of the people after the priest asked his question.

BOOK REVIEW: The question that wasn't a question.

WOLF HAAS: Nobody opened his mouth. Nobody said, "but Anni loves someone else," or anything like that. Just silence.

BOOK REVIEW: And some throat-clearing.

WOLF HAAS: The throat-clearing wasn't too bad. I exaggerated that a bit. I love throat-clearing when it starts in a room full of people. The contagiousness of it. This precursor to speech, as it were, this half-involuntary, half meaningful expression.

BOOK REVIEW: It says "The only thing that could be heard in response to the priest's question was, first, an isolated throat-clearing that then got louder and more frequent. But not the kind of throat-clearing that comes from an irrepressible objection, that precedes a public statement to make before a silent congregation, but rather more the embarrassed kind of throat-clearing that slips out of a group of people overcome by a moment of silence."

WOLF HAAS: Yes that's exactly how it was.

BOOK REVIEW: Did the throat-clearing really carry to the cemetery outside?

WOLF HAAS: To some extent. I think that throat-clearing and coughing have a frequency that broadcasts particularly well. Sometimes on a mobile phone you hear throat-clearing nearby, way too clearly.

BOOK REVIEW: I actually can't agree with you there. The loudest background noises on my mobile are always kids screaming and anything shrill.

WOLF HAAS: Yes, that's true actually. Maybe it was more perceivable than audible.

BOOK REVIEW: But you misunderstood my question. I didn't mean did the sound of the throat-clearing carry outside, but whether it was contagious and the people in the cemetery started clearing their throats.

WOLF HAAS: Oh. No! You don't clear your throat when you're out in the open. In the cemetery the priest's pause had the opposite effect. Only then did the people quiet down. Before that they'd been talking the whole time.

BOOK REVIEW: That's the reason people stay outside.

WOLF HAAS: Exactly. But now after the priest's embarrassing question, or command that was taken as an embarrassing question, outside it got quiet in the cemetery.

BOOK REVIEW: It's mostly the men who stay outside and send their wives and the churchy types in.

WOLF HAAS: Traditionally it's the men, sure. In the villages they always preferred to hold masses outdoors and to participate at the edges, so to speak, as cigarette smokers. Away from the watchful eyes of priests, women, and God. I think they probably made a lot of deals back then, and maybe they still do today.

BOOK REVIEW: The way businessmen in cities play golf so that in the clubhouse –

WOLF HAAS: Exactly! Because you can use the half-official atmosphere of the cemetery for all kinds of things. You know, a mixed bag: smoke a couple of cigarettes, sell a cow or a car, tell a joke, betray a friend, give a vacation tip.

BOOK REVIEW: At least trade a little bit of innuendo about the bride. You depict that with unmistakable pleasure.

WOLF HAAS: But that was before the priest's question. Of course there were still a few remarks, that much is clear. Thanks to the priest's request for someone to speak, they all fell silent! Suddenly it got quite silent in the cemetery and the men, like Olympic synchronized smokers, took refuge in a deep, simultaneous inhalation.

BOOK REVIEW: The impact of the explosion really comes across indirectly. At first you don't understand what happened when you're reading. You only experience it through this collective inhalation and through the pause in the mid- breath when the synchronized smokers are still holding it in. As if the men suddenly turned to stone. As though the smoke had frozen in their airways from fright.

WOLF HAAS: But I do mention the bang!

BOOK REVIEW: Sure, of course you do. It says that the

men staring in wonder and disbelief mistakenly thought the “apocalyptic thunder” was a celebratory firecracker from a fireworks display that had gone off too early. Even though their eyes saw the hill fly up into the air!

WOLF HAAS: Lift.

BOOK REVIEW: Lift?

WOLF HAAS: They see the hillside behind the high tension wires lift into the air, not fly. It’s more of an elegant, spaceship-like rising. That’s why the picture didn’t fit with the abrupt bang, somehow it wasn’t synchronized. Elegant appearance, brutal sound.

BOOK REVIEW: As we now well know, the sound wave of the thunder can come later. It’s actually not logical that the men in the cemetery took the bang for early fireworks, even though they’d seen the hillside lifted up into the air.

WOLF HAAS: The two things have to be differentiated. The men in the cemetery naturally saw the hillside lift up into air first, and then heard the boom afterward, but for the reader it’s the other way around. I don’t reveal yet what the men in the cemetery see. The readers just see their horrified wide-eyed faces. And then they hear the boom. Beforehand! Before they see the hillside lift into the air.

BOOK REVIEW: Yes, but in reality the people in the cemetery see the hillside lift into the air before they hear the boom!

WOLF HAAS: Naturally the thunder rolled in a couple seconds too late and also a little too briefly and too explosively, while their wide-open eyes had a good long glimpse of this poetic image of a hillside ascension, as it were.

BOOK REVIEW: And despite this, the men take the blast for early wedding fireworks! For me it's just about the fact that you can really study people's denial of reality in a situation of shock.

WOLF HAAS: You just don't want something like that to be true. You see it, and you don't believe it. That the mountain is rising up to heaven.

BOOK REVIEW: Whereas it was less the mountain *per se* than its contents.

WOLF HAAS: True. But that comes later, when the observers understand that image and sound go together. At first there is total disbelief and speechlessness.

BOOK REVIEW: But the terror of comprehension is released all the more powerfully. In the middle of this panic-stricken atmosphere of catastrophe they return to the priest's question. Well, I have to say, you were gutsy enough to write: "The screams of terror and disbelief that erupt from the people in the cemetery have nothing to do with the priest's charge to cry out now or forever hold your peace."

WOLF HAAS: (*laughs*) Yes, that's a good one. I have to give myself a pat on the back.

BOOK REVIEW: And then finally, after all that, comes the explanation for the reader. Only in the next sentence does it say, "The general horror of the churchyard-believers could be explained only by the overwhelming sight that met their crater-wide eyes. On the sunny hillside, right over the high tension wires, a volcano had erupted for the first time in recorded history."

WOLF HAAS: Do you think I laid it on too thick? I did get rid of the earthquake in the cemetery.

BOOK REVIEW: On the contrary. I think it's almost a shame how briefly you describe the actual sensation. You said before that the main effort you exerted in writing the book was changing narrative perspective. So, how could you show the hill exploding from the perspective of the wedding guests, even though the first-person narrator was still stuck in the mountain? You built the whole structure of the book around this problem. Hence the countdowns. The countdowns to the borders, the time-shifting surprises. The influence of volcanic eruptions on the weather.

WOLF HAAS: Yes.

BOOK REVIEW: The thing about this enormous effort that surprises me is that you almost give the event away.

WOLF HAAS: But it's described elaborately, how half the hill under the high tension wires flies up into the air.

BOOK REVIEW: Lifts.

WOLF HAAS: And the way the high tension pole shoots into the valley like an enormous Indian arrow.

BOOK REVIEW: That didn't make me think of Indians as much as the cyclops Polyphemus who throws his spear into the valley.

WOLF HAAS: And how the sky darkens because all of the things that Anni's father had been hoarding in the smuggler's den for years and years rise up into the sky, all the cheap radios and televisions and so on, how the stuff erupts all over the hillsides around the smuggler's den.

BOOK REVIEW: You get really poetic in this passage: "An enormous, hundred meter high geyser of televisions and fire extinguishers and folding chairs and cassette recorders, and wheel rims –"

WOLF HAAS. Yes, geyser. (*laughs)* Sometimes you can't say it any other way. Because that's the way it shot out, just like a . . . a fountain, and at the top, where the pressure wasn't as great it fanned out like an umbrella across the sky, or how should I describe it, like a cloud, and that's why it got dark. Because of all the coffee makers and heaters and tool boxes and tires and bumpers and immersion heaters and camp stoves and headlights and work benches and sets of dishes and record players and electric saws and refrigerators and I don't know what else.

BOOK REVIEW: Mr. Bonati seems to have been more passionate as a buyer than a seller.

WOLF HAAS: I think so too. The main reason for the overfilled storeroom was, of course, that he was torn from this life so abruptly.

BOOK REVIEW: Before he could sell.

WOLF HAAS: But you're right, anyway. There was years and years' worth of stuff stacked up there. I think he was almost more a collector than a smuggler.

BOOK REVIEW: As a smuggler he was the last in a long line. Almost like Kowalski's father, who was the first in his family not to be a miner. Both of them still had a sentimental attachments to these professions.

WOLF HAAS: That's true, actually. That's an interesting parallel. Mr. Bonati was, of course, more than a purely sentimental collector. But nonetheless, slightly kind of obsessed. He bought more than he sold.

BOOK REVIEW: You could also put it in a positive light. He was a businessman with integrity who was investing in the future when he accumulated all this stock.

WOLF HAAS: Yes, exactly, except that the junk didn't appreciate, it only fell in value.

BOOK REVIEW: And again, you list everything with particular glee. Sewing machines flying into the air, and lamps and bottles of motor oil and mirrors and rugs and mattresses and windshield wipers and drills and lawn mowers. It's crazy how much stuff he hoarded.

WOLF HAAS: Yes, whole clouds of tire chains and jigsaws and tractor tires and spin dryers and electric knives and slide projectors and calculators and cameras and vacuum cleaners and those old fashioned hairdryer helmets and electric razors and electric grills and car radios. A fountain of Revere ware pots and pans hand-held mixers and soldering irons and juicers and aluminum wheels and welding torches and clock radios and model trains and steam irons poured out over the whole south side of the hill.

BOOK REVIEW: The things you list – hand-held mixers, electric knives, clock radios and everything – that's all the detritus of affluence.

WOLF HAAS: Yes, affluent detritus. That's not entirely wrong. But you can't say that. It sounds kind of –

BOOK REVIEW: – stupid.

WOLF HAAS: Not stupid, but –

BOOK REVIEW: It seemed to me when I was reading that, for you it really was all about the leftovers of affluence. The list of things goes on for pages: the Bosch drills, the slotcar racetracks, the Remington hairdryers, the Olivetti typewriters, the Braun shavers, the Mauser machine guns, the Allibert medicine cabinets, the Philips radios, the Kenwood deep fat fryers, the Moulinex food graters, the Siemens vacuum cleaners, the tailpipes, or exhausts, what do you call them?

WOLF HAAS: Exhausts – exhaust pipes – hmm. I don't know. Exhausts, right?

BOOK REVIEW: The wheel rims, the tires, the school bags, the record players, the slide projectors, the pressure cookers, the soldering irons, the calculators, the tile cutters, the stereo equipment, the mangles. It sounds as if all the items in an enormous department store are exploding.

WOLF HAAS: There's an explanation for that. First, he died before he could sell the goods.
BOOK REVIEW: But so much! You get the feeling that the volcano shoots more goods into the air than could ever fit into the storeroom.

WOLF HAAS: That's what the book is about! That so many things are left behind when a person dies. Everything stays behind, even when the person isn't a smuggler.

BOOK REVIEW: That's what the book is about for you?

WOLF HAAS: Well, "about" is a little exaggerated. But this is a passage where, in retrospect, I wouldn't cut anything. Now if I were working on the manuscript I couldn't say, drills in, jigsaws out, soldering iron in, slide projector out, iron, cassette recorder, and Revere ware pot in, juicer and electric grill out.

BOOK REVIEW: Why not?

WOLF HAAS: I couldn't do it. I just listed everything. I swiped the list from the local officer in charge of the clean-up.

BOOK REVIEW: You just listed everything?

WOLF HAAS: Yes, that's the trick. The more massive a list is, the more you believe it represents a selection, and the items listed stand for countless unlisted ones. But in reality, that's all there was. The list didn't take up more than four and a half standard size sheets of paper, all totaled up. Waste paper basket (2), work gloves (3 packs of 100, one open, 9 missing), rechargeable battery (10), baby monitor (5), stapler (57), and so on, that's the way the officer wrote it up. Stapler could go under S, or under O for office supplies. Hole punch wasn't listed under H, but under P for Paper hole punch. They wrote it up alphabetically, ending with zither.

BOOK REVIEW: That could have gone under "I" for instrument.

WOLF HAAS: Or "M" for musical instrument. And I have the suspicion that Mr. Bonati didn't smuggle the zither, but had it up there in the love nest to serenade Mrs. Kowalski now and then.

BOOK REVIEW: She even mentions that in one of the letters.

WOLF HAAS: Exactly.

BOOK REVIEW: Quick question. Some of Mrs. Kowalski's letters were found during the cleanup. They didn't find any of his?

WOLF HAAS: No. Naturally there weren't any in the smuggler's den. Makes sense. But Vittorio also didn't find any at home. Honestly, though, I think Bonati didn't write that much. I don't want to say something I can't prove, but I can imagine that, well, how should I put this –

BOOK REVIEW: – that Mrs. Kowalski wasn't the only woman to visit the smuggler's den.

WOLF HAAS: As I said, I don't know. I'm just going on what I heard.

BOOK REVIEW: His collecting wasn't restricted to contraband.

WOLF HAAS: I don't think he was that much of a notorious womanizer either. He was just an average guy.

BOOK REVIEW: Ah –

WOLF HAAS: In any case, not a neurotic world record-holder like Riemer.

BOOK REVIEW: And Lukki?

WOLF HAAS: Well, then there's Lukki. You can't blame him. He had never been married before.

BOOK REVIEW: And now he still isn't. His rival Kowalski gave an emphatic answer to the priest's question, if anyone had just cause why Anni and Lukki shouldn't be joined in marriage.

WOLF HAAS: But nobody knew it at the time. I mean, that it was Vittorio Kowalski who had given the answer. For the people who were standing outside it was the mountain that answered and prevented the vows from taking place.

BOOK REVIEW: The volcano.

WOLF HAAS: And the boom was worse for the people in the church, because it was amplified, and the colored stained glass windows that had cast that beautiful light on Anni shattered and let the harsh daylight in. At that moment, they saw for the first time how beautiful the weather outside was!

BOOK REVIEW: For the people in the church the thunderclap was completely inexplicable, because they hadn't seen anything of the volcanic eruption.

WOLF HAAS: That's why it was an even more

menacing answer to the priest's question, almost like the rumbling of God. Anyway, it would have been unthinkable to continue with the ceremony.

BOOK REVIEW: Instead, everyone rushed outside. But you don't really describe it as panic. It sounds very orderly.

WOLF HAAS: Yes, an orderly panic, if there is such a thing.

BOOK REVIEW: I would say there isn't. The definition of panic is complete disorder.

WOLF HAAS: Maybe the same group of people would have flown into a panic if they'd been penned up in an inn or ballroom – well, in more of a raucous place – and the earth shook and the glass in the windows shattered. But I think a church radiates a kind of orderly authority.

BOOK REVIEW: You're saying that the spiritual aura curbed the panic?

WOLF HAAS: The spiritual aura was just part of it. The rigid architecture is the other. The immovable pews where twenty people sit next to each other in a row. They can only leave one at a time, through the eye of the needle so to speak. That adds a sense of discipline. That's different from an inn, where people shove tables and chairs squeaking and creaking across the floor and really make a racket. Besides, it's a practice that's lasted for years and centuries, this filing out of the authoritarian pews.

BOOK REVIEW: In the book it says "like a many-headed caterpillar."

WOLF HAAS: Well, anyway even in a normal scenario it's really tough because each person genuflects quickly when leaving the pew and entering the aisle.

BOOK REVIEW: But they skipped the genuflection.

WOLF HAAS: (*laughs*) That was the panic! They left without genuflecting!

BOOK REVIEW: And without crossing themselves.

WOLF HAAS: I don't know about that. I can imagine that a few people crossed themselves. But in any case they pushed their way out in an orderly fashion. In reverse order of their importance at the wedding because the most important people were up in the front of the church.

BOOK REVIEW: Now suddenly the last row has the better position.

WOLF HAAS: Naturally they were the first ones out, long before the relatives and the bridal couple. And, as unfair as it is, the ones who weren't in the church were best off. Those standing in the cemetery were the first to run up the mountain. Behind them came the standing-room-only people, the half-hearted ones that milled around in the entrance, behind them the acquaintances of the bride in the very last rows, then the friends and the distant relatives who were sitting in the middle of the church.

BOOK REVIEW: And then only after them, the close relatives.

WOLF HAAS: It took them forever to push out of the first rows to the church door, and finally to fight their way out into the open. Behind the relatives came the close family, and behind the family the witnesses, and behind the witnesses, the bride and groom, and, not until they were out, the priest and altar boys.

BOOK REVIEW: And finally, the poor choir.

WOLF HAAS: Yes, of course they were last. They had the longest way from the gallery down to the exit, that much is clear.

BOOK REVIEW: In contrast to the people in the cemetery, the people in the church still had no idea what actually happened.

WOLF HAAS: Nada! Only as they ran up the steep path behind the others to the smuggler's den, did they see that the mountain had spit out all the contraband from long-forgotten years and decades and spread it out over the meadows and fields in an area of several square kilometers.

BOOK REVIEW: But Lukki, the alpha-male, manages to fight his way to the front of the human caterpillar despite his bad starting position.

WOLF HAAS: I didn't necessarily want to identify him as an alpha-male.

BOOK REVIEW: But that's how it comes across. You always compare him to Anni's father.

WOLF HAAS: Yes, maybe, but he was the head of the mountain rescue team.

BOOK REVIEW: Just like Anni's father.

WOLF HAAS: And as such he had to fight his way to the front. It was his job, so to speak.

BOOK REVIEW: Do you think he was the only one who had an idea how the explosion had happened?

WOLF HAAS: No, I don't think so. Not Lukki. Anni, maybe.

BOOK REVIEW: Yes, of course. With her "terror feeling"?

WOLF HAAS: That's really bugging you! In any case, Lukki acted in an incredibly concentrated way. It took him almost the whole way up the path to get to the front of the procession. At the first bench he was still way down below; at the second bench he got to the middle, because everyone was running. Up the mountain! But then he was the first to get to the top. If he suspected anything, it was that despite the destruction, it could still be a matter of life and death. He kept barking "Careful, careful, careful!" so people didn't get too close to the crater.

BOOK REVIEW: He even said it before he got to the top, "there's got to be somebody under there."

WOLF HAAS: Definitely. But I don't think he thought it was Kowalski.

BOOK REVIEW: Lukki's first words when he got to the edge of the crater were: "Maybe he's still alive!"

WOLF HAAS: Yes. But it was just a sort of general "he." You just say that. He always had to think about the survivors, although it didn't seem there'd be any here. Nonetheless, he did what he'd been taught to do. With cave-ins, no matter how it might look, you have to think about survivors. He immediately started doing knocking signals. *Tock tock tock.*

BOOK REVIEW: At this point your story breaks off abruptly.

WOLF HAAS: You can't say that. The end is at the beginning, as I said. Vittorio Kowalski wakes up in the hospital and finally gets his first kiss from Anni. The one he'd been working toward for fifteen years.

BOOK REVIEW: A happy ending.

WOLF HAAS: Do I hear a cynical tone in your voice?

BOOK REVIEW: I'm not cynical. But you kind of neglect Lukki's death during the rescue.

WOLF HAAS: Really? While I was writing I got the feeling like, now you're pushing it again.

BOOK REVIEW: No! I didn't even get it the first time I read that Lukki saved the buried man and lost his own life in the process.

WOLF HAAS: Yes, but you can't accompany something like that with a string orchestra. That would be unbearable. That's why I completely neglected to draw parallels between this and the mining accidents, although it strongly suggested itself, because a lot of times the rescue team gets killed in an accident while the buried person survives.

BOOK REVIEW: I don't want to sound schoolmarmish here. On the contrary, I think it's really interesting how the reader becomes an accomplice. You hope that Anni and Vittorio will get together, and the nuisance should just somehow go away.

WOLF HAAS: Well, who the nuisance is has to do with the narrative perspective. In Kowalski's love story, Lukki is the nuisance; to that extent it's true about the reader's being an accomplice. But in reality, in that village Lukki is the deserving one.

BOOK REVIEW: The top dog.

WOLF HAAS: And Kowalski is the intruder. The nuisance who should make himself scarce – disappear back to the Ruhr.

BOOK REVIEW: Slink away.

WOLF HAAS: Exactly. So things take their ordained course.

BOOK REVIEW: But Vittorio Kowalski wasn't going away.

WOLF HAAS: He protected himself.

BOOK REVIEW: That's really the only reason you root for him. And that you don't really take the grieving for the top dog quite so seriously, even though he was his savior.

WOLF HAAS: Yes, definitely. There's something about

weaklings striking back. He really fought tooth and nail for Anni.

BOOK REVIEW: First he disposed of Anni's father, and then her groom.

WOLF HAAS: And now he finally gets his first kiss.

BOOK REVIEW: That he waited fifteen years for.

WOLF HAAS: And it's so good!

BOOK REVIEW: Two centimeters in a straight line from the corner of his left eye.

WOLF HAAS: Yes. He feels it all night long. He was so afraid that the kiss would fade that he didn't dare move in his hospital bed until the morning.

BOOK REVIEW: Judging by the force of the explosion, he got off pretty easy with his injuries.

WOLF HAAS: A bad concussion, broken arm. That's not nothing, but –

BOOK REVIEW: – that will heal.

WOLF HAAS: You comfort kids by telling them "it will get better – until you get married." He was really lucky. Except of course they never found the toe during the clean-up.

BOOK REVIEW: But the only thing he feels that night is his cheekbone.

WOLF HAAS: Yes, it's inflamed, as it were. He doesn't

think about anything else. He just wants the kiss to stay on his cheek until Anni comes to visit him again tomorrow. She even said, tomorrow I'll come back.

BOOK REVIEW: By the end I was waiting the whole time for him to remember.

WOLF HAAS: What do you mean, remember?

BOOK REVIEW: That was probably too vague for you, I understand. But somehow when you're reading, you miss the resolution. If only the memory had come to him in bits and pieces. Maybe when he wakes up in the hospital or something. Or after the kiss, as he guards it through the night, the memory could have come back then.

WOLF HAAS: I'm not really sure what you're getting at.

BOOK REVIEW: Come on. What am I getting at? His silver star orgasm.

WOLF HAAS: I was really curious to find out why you put your watch on the other wrist.

BOOK REVIEW: Right, I can put it back now. I really would have beaten myself up later if I had forgotten to ask you about that.

WOLF HAAS: It's a little bit like the priest at the wedding. When it comes down to it, you really haven't asked me anything.

BOOK REVIEW: The question is, why are you so coyly silent about the fact that, because of his silver star orgasm, he forgot for fifteen years what really happened between him and Anni in the smuggler's den while Anni's father was being washed away to his death in the valley.

WOLF HAAS: Well, that's news to me. I even wrote that he'd never been with a woman –

BOOK REVIEW: Sure, sure. You also wrote that after a silver star orgasm you can't remember anything.

WOLF HAAS: Well, okay. Then you can just go ahead and assume anything you like. You could say that about anybody, "you had a silver star orgasm, you just can't remember it."

BOOK REVIEW: But the evidence in the text is really more explicit.

WOLF HAAS: This is precisely the reason I didn't write a detective story, and you're coming at me with evidence.

BOOK REVIEW: You really can't maintain this romanticized version of "just a kiss." I thought it was to your credit that you leave it to the reader to come up with this. It can be really tiring when everything is explained in a text.

WOLF HAAS: In principle, I don't leave anything up to the reader.

BOOK REVIEW: But only through the silver star orgasm that robbed fifteen-year-old Vittorio Kowalski of his senses for the first and last time does the text gain closure. No man stays under the spell of a woman for fifteen years because of an abruptly interrupted kiss.

WOLF HAAS: Kiss, well – and lying naked in the hay! I write that.

BOOK REVIEW: Cuddling in the hay doesn't cut it either! You intend to tell me in all seriousness that you write pages about Riemer's silver star theory in your novel, that you publicize the sexual secrets of Vittorio's late mother without trying to get at anything. That would be like, if nobody ever shot Chekhov's famous musket that was leaning against the wall in the first act.

WOLF HAAS: I would like to have one interview where this Chekhov weapon isn't mentioned.

BOOK REVIEW: Besides, Vittorio couldn't have bumped off Anni's father with a kiss. That's really –

WOLF HAAS: Right, it's a bit disproportionate. That got to me too. It would have been better if it had happened during their "*first time.*"

BOOK REVIEW: What do you mean, would have? The whole text is teeming with clues that the son inherited his penchant for passionate devotion from his mother.

WOLF HAAS: Do you think that can be inherited? A kind of sexual mistake in the genetic code?

BOOK REVIEW: What I think is irrelevant right now. But your text does teem with – I've got to say, broad hints! You don't have Vittorio Kowalski tell about the critical minutes in the smuggler's den after the two of them are lying stark naked in the steaming hay.

WOLF HAAS: He's a discreet guy. That is certainly not a broad hint.

BOOK REVIEW: The broad hint of the eloquent silence. Kowalski acts as though nothing happened but knocking signals.

WOLF HAAS: He talks about knocking signals because that was the decisive thing in this situation.

BOOK REVIEW: But I also think the knocking signals were the decisive thing here. Except they were completely different knocking signals, that even a sexually naïve deaf person could hear in this novel.

WOLF HAAS: Well, I'm really starting to fear that you can hear the grass grow.

BOOK REVIEW: Erupting volcanoes, the penetrating *tock tock tock,* these are all things that have nothing to do with kissing, Mr. Haas.

WOLF HAAS: No, well, the knocking signals weren't meant that way. That would be embarrassing.

BOOK REVIEW: I don't understand why you won't just admit it. Are you afraid that people will assume you have some kind of defloration complex? Then you shouldn't have written the book. Mr. Haas, what happened in those minutes, when Mr. Bonati was hammering on the locked entrance to his smuggler's den in a panic? What transpired between the two children?

WOLF HAAS: Okay then. If you really want to know, I can reveal how it really was. But you have to turn off the tape recorder.

BOOK REVIEW: Oh, you can just tell me like this. I'll just leave it out if you don't want me to print it.

WOLF HAAS: You should probably turn it off, so I can really tell you everything.

BOOK REVIEW: Okay. But definitely remind me to turn it back on when we talk about Mrs. Ba-

Afterword
by
Thomas S. Hansen

Wolf Haas was born in 1960 in Maria Alm am Steinernen Meer, a small village in the province of Salzburg, Austria. After receiving his diploma in 1978 from boarding school in the city of Salzburg, he entered the University of Salzburg, where he studied psychology for two years and linguistics and German for the second two. After a two-year stint as a university lecturer in Swansea, Wales, Haas returned to Austria to work as a copy-editor for the advertising firm Demner and Merlicek. There he advanced quickly, producing successful slogans for radio and print campaigns. Two of his most inventive exhibit the talent for wordplay that would later characterize his literary work: "*Lichtfahrer sind sichtbarer*" ("drivers who use running lights are more visible") and "*Öl gehört gehört*" ("Ö1" [network] deserves to be heard).

Haas's reputation as one of Austria's most popular authors rests primarily on the cult status of his "Detective Brenner" crime novels. These six volumes present the exploits of a cantankerous ex-cop plagued by migraines. The books use vernacular Austrian expressions, both in dialogue and the breezy, colloquial narrative, in which the authorial voice addresses the reader in the familiar, "*du,*" form. This stylistic trait creates a bond between narrator and reader, even as the general tone distances the novels from the standard literary language of High German. The Brenner novels were originally rejected by German publishers, not least because of the colloquial style that later made them famous. Brenner's death in the sixth book of the series closed a creative era for Haas, in which he mastered one literary form and prepared to take a new direction.

The Weather Fifteen Years Ago, his first departure from the crime novel, was published in German in 2006. In it, Haas playfully evokes postmodern literary games – all of the characters and plot of the story emerge in dialogue, teasing, and argument between a fictional German book reviewer and a (fictional?) Austrian writer called "Wolf Haas." Their dialogue is witty, colloquial, occasionally irascible, and didactic (about Austrian colloquialisms and culture, primarily). In the course of their conversation and wrangling, all details of plot and character emerge, as it were, in palimpsest. The story they describe (and which the reader must infer) includes classic, even melodramatic, surprises and plot twists common in popular mysteries and love stories. Lovers, who met as children, reunite after years of separation, on the eve of the female character's wedding to another man.

Haas's fascination with German-Austrian tensions and linguistic differences infuse the work. From the outset of the five-part interview, the North German interviewer and the Austrian author mirror the lovers in the fictitious novel they discuss. The German protagonist, Vittorio Kowalski (his name shows Haas's playfulness), hails from the industrial Ruhr region, famous for mining and occasional mining disasters. His love interest, Anni, comes from a tiny village in the Austrian Alps where the Kowalski family vacationed every summer of the children's youth. Just as in the interview between the reviewer and author, nationality, regional vocabulary, and cultural references enliven the communication between the young lovers in their reported dialogue.

Austrian writers have often felt the need to distinguish their literary language from High German. Publishers occasionally apply pressure to standardize their style and minimize local linguistic idiosyncrasies in the name of popular appeal. In *The Weather Fifteen Years Ago*, Haas plays with this tension. Austria and Germany are (as the adage about the U.S. and Great Britain states) two cultures separated by the same language. To be sure, these linguistic nuances can get lost in translation. An example is the interviewer's North German pronunciation of words like "ürgendwie" and "Kürche," which sound so foreign to Austrian ears. The juxtaposition of Austrian and German idioms produce humor as the speakers sometimes misunderstand each other, but as the interview proceeds, cross-cultural understanding grows deeper as the plot of the non-existent novel takes shape though their dialogue.

The form of this experimental novel deserves some explanation. Critics have labeled *The Weather Fifteen Years Ago* "metafiction," a post-modernist concept that denotes literary strategies that foreground narration itself rather than narrative elements like plot and characters. Post-modern literature revels in devices that explicitly interrupt the story line to divert the reader from the content to the form of the fiction. These self-analytical devices present the reader with a critical voice (or voices) that exists outside and above the narrative, while simultaneously forming part of it. Haas uses this post-modern technique to present a story entirely by implication, forcing the reader to collaborate with the author and construct a narrative of the imagination. Haas locates his work squarely in the distinguished tradition of metafiction as represented by Vladimir Nabokov's *Pale Fire* (1962), in which the story emerges in foot-notes to a poem. Similarly, Jorge Luis Borges delighted in reviewing nonexistent books that must be inferred by the reader's imagination.

All metafiction confronts readers with clearly playful literary experiences. Haas chooses to do more than interrupt a plot line with meta-narrative or digression; he presents the whole narrative in this form. The result produces some intriguing puzzles to engage readers in constructing their own interpretations and even alternative story lines. The often argumentative conversation between the fictional author and the interviewer, in which they disagree about interpretation and even plot, establishes the unreliability of any narrative point of view. “Haas” claims to tell Vittorio Kowalski’s quest for love, and in doing so, he betrays an identification with his character so close that at one point the third person and first person pronouns merge: the narrator’s “he” (describing Kowalski) slips into “I.” To add to this shifting point of view, the time levels in the tale are also porous. The narrated sequence of events does not unfold chronologically but emerges according to the associative vagaries of interviewer and author – and both comment on this fact. Time is almost an exercise in *praeteritio,* which is driven by disclaimers like “we won’t mention the fact that . . .” or “I’ve cut a certain passage.” These strategies themselves generate new content and propel the reader through various associative digressions toward the dramatic climax.

Unreliability also describes Haas’s own fictional persona within the work. His identity is so slippery that at certain points readers may ask, “just who is narrating the story?” Although several references ally him with the author of Wolf Haas’s own books, this post-modern persona is less autobiographical than a fictional character who overidentifies with the story of Anni and Vittorio, thereby blurring the boundaries between narrative and narration.

Despite its pervasive, playful experimentation, however, *The Weather Fifteen Years Ago* is firmly grounded in reality and in places almost revels in genuine, highly specialized scientific and technical information. The protagonist is not only an engineer, fascinated with details of meteorology and statistics; he is also the descendant of generations of coal miners, imbued with details of their work, equipment, and tales of terrifying mining disasters. In addition, *Das Wetter* is an intensely Austrian novel, full of authentic cultural references to Alpine topography, historical events, and even contemporary writers like Christoph Ransmayr, Raoul Schrott, and Peter Handke. Readers familiar with Austrian culture will recognize, and perhaps be amused by, the clichés, or – like the German interviewer – they may find the narrator instructing them about their meanings. As the title proclaims, Haas establishes a further substratum of concreteness by packing his text with facts and terms from meteorology. Played off against a secondary association of the word "*Wetter*" that relates to mining, this level creates an increasingly dense web of parallels and contradictions for readers to savor. Whereas the alpine weather (*das Wetter*) and the act of climbing mountains (*Steigen*) determine life in Anni's alpine region, in Vittorio's homeland in the Ruhr the local term *Wettersteiger* denotes mining engineers who monitor the tunnel ventilation (*Grubenbewetterung*) in the mines. Thus, life deep in the (German) earth of Vittorio's homeland inversely mirrors conditions on the high mountain peaks of Anni's (Austrian) homeland. The two realms merge explosively – literally – in the climax of the story. And even after the reader understands both the drama and the joke, the fictitious author and nonexistent reviewer imply that they are about to reveal another tantalizing detail to the story. But as the interviewer turns the tape off and deprives readers of the author's explanation, we are left alone to confront the mystery at the heart of the narrative.

CPSIA information can be obtained
at www.ICGtesting.com
Printed in the USA
FSOW01n1517230315
5849FS

9 781572 411661